LOST AND Found

PALMETTO
PUBLISHING
Charleston, SC
www.PalmettoPublishing.com

Paperback ISBN: 979-8-8229-1850-4
eBook ISBN: 979-8-8229-3503-7

ONE DAY YOUR WORST NIGHTMARE COULD
TURN INTO YOUR MOST CHERISHED DREAM

LOST AND Found

by Mattie Hill

Dedication

This story is dedicated to all the parents, siblings, grandparents, and other family members that, due to circumstances beyond their control, did not have the privilege of creating endearing life memories with their loved one. These memories are the core foundation that binds and holds families together.

This story's intent was not to reflect poorly on any of the characters in my narrative. The goal was simply to write about my journey, which in turn allowed me to develop hope for the future and aid in the healing of wounds long held raw.

So many of my family and friends have traveled with me on this journey. However, there is one person that was always there for me through my venting and tear-filled phone calls and texts. That person is my sister. She became my best friend, and the keeper of my darkest secrets. Yet, through all my ranting, she was one of the most positive influences on how to once again regain the Mattie Hill that existed before this journey. Carole, your support has known no bounds, and I cherish you with all my heart.

Finally, this is dedicated to my grandson, Jeremy. The five years of memories are far too few but so very precious. I hold on to them as a daily reminder of our special bond. One day, my boy, we will meet again and enjoy making new memories together.

Although based in part on a true story, this is predominantly a work of fiction. Any resemblance to actual persons, living or dead, or actual events is purely coincidental.

In closing, please don't hesitate to reach out to your loved ones, near or far, close to you or distant. For they, too, may need to heal, just as you do.

Grief, I've learned, is just love. It's all the love you want to give but cannot. All that unspent love gathers up in the corners of your eyes, the lump in your throat, and in that hollow part of your chest. Grief is just love with no place to go.

—Jamie Anderson

Prologue

It was morning again, and my eyes crusted with the lack of sleep, try to open from another fretful and interrupted night. Like a scratched recording, day and night, it's a repeat of the same awful notes. I try to return to a dream state, but honestly, all I do is rest, or rest in repose, almost as if I am in a coffin, surrounded not with soft satin and pillows but with a lifetime of aborted memories that literally stopped me from living so many years ago.

And that's how I feel all the time, every day, every hour: in a casket that is clamped down tightly with no air to breathe and covered with dark, dank earth, weighing down my soul with absolutely no chance of escape. "Why is this, you ask?" The answer is simple. I lost my sweet boy.

I toss the sweat-stained and wrinkled sheets aside and think, "Another day…another day of nothingness." As I sit up on the edge of the bed, I shuffle into my slippers and move the nearly empty bottle of Merlot to the far side of my cluttered nightstand that is filled with bottles of meds prescribed to make me feel better, normal, or to help me sleep. None of them work.

Looking down at my nightstand, I realize that the top drawer is slightly ajar. Pulling the drawer fully open, I pull out my 22-caliber and notice that there is a full clip loaded. "Shit, I must have loaded it last night when I was drinking my fifth or sixth glass of wine, or maybe my eighth! Not a smart thing to do," I chastise myself.

I place the still-loaded weapon on my nightstand and stare at it for a few more seconds.

As I finish getting my slippers on my wrinkled and veined old feet, I shuffle to the bathroom for my daily morning routine of hygiene: pee, brush my teeth, floss between the teeth that are still mine, and comb some semblance of order into my unruly curly gray hair.

Walking toward my bed to put the sheets and blankets in order, I glance back at the .22. Moving to the nightstand, I pick up the weapon, ready to release the clip from the weapon, and I suddenly realize something.

I realize I am tired. Really and overwhelmingly tired. I am tired of the life that I have had to live over the last fifteen years, and I am exhausted trying to reconcile with myself as to why it all happened to begin with.

"What the hell," I say to myself. "I'm old, and nothing is going to change. I still don't have my boy in my life, so what do I have that's worth living for?"

I grab the weapon, release the safety, and put my finger on the trigger. I close my weary eyes and raise my arm, fully prepared to end this never-ending cycle.

Taking a deep breath, I begin to squeeze the trigger smoothly, as my husband, David, had taught me so many years ago down on the farm. Somewhere in my mental fog—due to the lack of sleep or too much wine and pharmaceuticals the night before—I hear a loud bang!

"Okay, I should not be feeling a thing. I know I squeezed the trigger, so why am I still standing, and why do I still hear that damn banging? Good Lord, did I screw this up too?"

The noise continues, and I realize that, first, I have failed at shooting my brains out and second, that someone is furiously knocking on my front door.

I put the safety back on the weapon, remove the clip, and place it back in the drawer. Before getting up to answer the unrelenting knocking, I look at the weapon and think, "I'll see you soon."

Pulling on an old sweater over my pj's, I go to the front door. Peering out, I see a UPS deliveryman. "What in the world does he want, and what is he delivering?" I wonder.

Leaving the chain on the front door, since at my age I don't trust anyone, I open the door slightly. "Good morning. Are you Mrs. Hill?" he asks.

"Yes, I am," I reply.

"I have an overnight delivery that requires your signature," he states. He holds out his handheld electronic device for my signature, and I sign it. He hands me the envelope through the chained door, saying, "Have a good day," as he retreats down my sidewalk.

I don't even acknowledge his comment. I shut my front door, lock it, and think to myself, "Yeah, right. Have a good day: not recently."

I don't even look at who the delivery is from, and I don't even care as I drop it on the other pile of miscellaneous correspondence that has accumulated on my hall table. Shuffling down the hallway back to my bedroom, I climb back into my cocoon of crumpled sheets and blankets, grab a sleeping pill, and swallow it with a sip of leftover wine. Ready to waste another day, I quickly fall into a restless sleep of dreams of a life that could have been. This time I hope my dreams allow me to experience a different outcome; if only myself and others had made different decisions in the past. Maybe if I had stopped being so controlling, things would have been okay.

As my worn-out body begins to fall into a *slightly* drug induced sleep—just slightly drug induced, may I add—my eyelids flutter closed, and I begin to dream. My dream begins with so much darkness that I feel like I'm a participant in Botticelli's painting interpretation of Dante's poem *Inferno*. I'm clawing my way to the top of the painting for some glimmer of light, some ray of hope. In my half-conscious state, I sense, but do not see, a presence so pure that I must get closer. It is a light that feels like life, love, family: everything that I had lost when I lost my boy. I have a brief sense of happiness. And then it vanishes just as quickly as it had emerged.

"Where has my light gone?" I wonder in my fantasy-dream state. I must find it again.

I struggle to claw over the "Dante dead" to get a glimpse of it, to once again feel that brief sense of happiness and peace. I plead to the dream gods. "Please let me see that light of peace one more time." I extend my arm, reaching and hoping that I can just get a bit closer and find that sweet glow again. Then, there it is, a glimmer of light on the horizon. I sense myself struggling to travel to the light.

As I grasp for the light, my dream sends me falling into a raging ocean that pulls my body down by its wicked current. Down I go into the dark, cold water beneath the waves. As I fight to reach the surface and escape the murky gloom that surrounds me, I glance down to see an apparition of a broken soul riding the wild currents that surround my body. In shock I realize that the watery vision is me.

Not wanting any part of that specter near me, I beg of myself, "Please wake up, old woman! Look up and keep heading for that light. It holds the answer. It holds the answer to heal your shattered soul. Once you find it, you'll wake up."

So, I keep going, wrestling to the surface, hoping to see that sliver of light, that flicker of hope and happiness. Perhaps, somehow, that glow will answer the question that I have asked myself countless times over the last several decades: "What did I do wrong to lose a child that I loved so dearly? A child that was my heart and soul."

And then it happens. I can't find the shining orb that I so desperately crave, and my dream engulfs me. I am pulled back down into a torrent of angry waves. Lightning flashes and dances on the dark canvas of the nightmare sky above me, and as pellets of rain plummet down, I feel myself dragged into a deep abyss. It is an abyss of heartache and loss. The waves continue to build above me, and I am hurled within them and eventually thrown onto an unknown shore by the sheer strength of this fantasy storm.

As I lie on the damp sand, exhausted, the storm begins to recede. My subconscious continues to wrestle me awake, and finally, as I open my eyes, I know that, somehow, I must change this horrible cycle. I need to tell my story and write it all down. Perhaps then my mind will be clear of all the bad memories so the good ones will surface to the forefront, and I again may be able enjoy what time I have left on this earth.

Fully awake now, and determined to put my demons to rest, I get up and stagger to my office to boot up my faithful old iMac to begin writing my story. Even before I put my fingers on the keyboard, words cascade through my mind, a powerful waterfall of memories and emotions. "This is exactly what I need to be doing," I think to myself. "This may finally heal me. I must rise to this challenge and tell our story. The story of you and me; the story of Nana and Jeremy."

Yet before I was Nana, I was Mattie. So let me take a moment to introduce you to her.

Chapter 1

One of the first memories of my mother was listening to
her recite Henry Wadsworth Longfellow to me:

There was a little girl,
Who had a little curl,
Right in the middle of her forehead.
When she was good, she was very, very good,
But when she was bad, she was horrid.

Was I a horrid child? Not very often.

Did I have a curl in the middle of my forehead? Always.

Who was that rarely horrid little girl with the little
curl right in the middle of her forehead?

It was me: Mattie Hill, to be precise; better known back then as Mattie Carroll.

The youngest of three children, I was the "oops baby" that arrived late in my parents' lives. Since I somehow had the foresight to be born late, I never witnessed the budget constraints that the rest of my siblings experienced growing up.

When I was an adolescent, my parents bought a beautiful four-bedroom colonial home in a well-established waterfront community. My sister, Carole, and my brother, Steven, both much older, left the nest shortly after we moved in. It was then that I essentially became an only child and began to reap the benefits of being that lucky child born late in my parents' lives.

Our neighbors were engineers, doctors, military officers, lawyers, and such. Since my father was a retired military officer, they fit right in with the neighbors. It also allowed me to attend the same school as the other children.

If I expressed an interest in music, art, sailing, or tennis, they would quickly grant my wish by buying a sailboat or a musical instrument or sending me to a tennis camp. However, my parents didn't send me to art camp since I displayed talent in that arena even as a young girl. No need to waste money.

My mom and dad loved to travel, and they would take me on all their trips to Europe, Yucatan and the east coast tropics.

It was a fabulous way to grow up. Having been afforded all these opportunities made me a very well-rounded young lady. Most of my friends fit into the same mold. We were all well-traveled, well versed in the arts and exposed to numerous appropriate pastimes for girls of that time. Yet, for me, it was very boring. So, I cured my boredom by becoming a daredevil of sorts.

If you were to ask my friends from my teenage days what I was like, they would all chorus the reply, "Never challenge Mattie to do anything, because she'll do it."

From jumping into the community pool fully clothed in the middle of winter, to climbing out a second-floor bedroom window and shimmying down a tree to go to a party, I did it. Didn't everybody accept a dare at least once or twice in their lifetime? Especially as a teenager?

Yeah, you still remember those dares, don't you?

On the other hand, if you asked my siblings the same question, the first thing out of their mouths would be that I was spoiled. And I was.

Yet buried deep inside me was a different Mattie, one that was struggling to emerge. Although I loved the life my parents provided me, I was constantly fighting the road that they wanted me to travel. They wanted me to follow their traditional path, the one that would lead me to marry an engineer, doctor, military officer, or lawyer.

I acquiesced to my parents' accepted wardrobe, complete with the turtleneck, small-wale cords, and argyle sweater, which I would casually drape around my shoulders and skillfully knot in the front so that it hung just right. I would complete my ensemble with a coordinating ribbon adorning my curly ponytail and the string of pearls that my godmother gave me. I looked like I had just walked off the pages of *The Official Preppy Handbook* that was so popular in my early teens.

Oh, just to let you know, the turtleneck, cords and sweater—that was the same outfit I wore when I jumped into the community pool all those years ago. I admit it was a tad heavy when wet, but thankfully I have always been a strong swimmer.

Inside, though, the budding rebel desperately struggled to emerge.

As I entered my mid-teens, that's exactly what happened. I became the daughter who no longer conformed to my family's ideologies, which were so traditional that my family still believed that the only acceptable fields of study for women were nursing, teaching, or the convent!

The convent certainly wasn't for me. They would never have accepted me as a novitiate, especially given what I had participated in as a teenager.

They believed that the Roman Catholic Church was the one and only true religion. If you celebrated a service at another denomination, you needed to go to confession afterward before you attended mass again. They watched *All in the Family* and laughed heartily when Archie spouted his racist remarks. But to be fair, that was the norm for upper middle-class families back then.

That lifestyle did not fit the newly developing Mattie.

As I entered my middle teenage years, I began to transition more to my true inner self. I no longer sported turtlenecks, pearls, and argyle sweaters. My clothing attire became tie-dyed hip-huggers, halter tops, platform shoes, and blue nail polish, with feather earrings gracing my double-pierced ears. My parents and my siblings began to shake their heads in horror when they saw me.

I loved every minute of it. I was finding myself, and I was forming my own opinions of the world around me and how I wanted to fit into that world. The Mattie I wanted to be was a Mattie that was independent of others' expectations and perfectly capable of being comfortable with that direction and its consequences. I wanted to be a woman who, if life threw her challenges, would be able to persevere and rise above those obstacles.

Don't get me wrong, I loved my family, and they loved me. But as I grew into my new beliefs, conflict also grew between myself and my parents.

My mother would often pull me aside and say, "You need to behave. You need to stop wearing those disgraceful clothes. It is not acceptable. And when did you get your ears pierced twice? My friends are talking, and your father is furious with you! You were not raised this way." I would listen and nod, but only to keep the peace. I suppose I just wasn't ready for the challenge of disagreeing with my mom or my stern father.

Truth be told, those admonishments from my mother and the silence from my father only made me more determined to be the unbridled me. My parents, however, had another plan. They sent me to an all-girls college in the mountains filled with girls in the turtlenecks, pearls, and argyle sweaters that I had abandoned. I suppose they were hoping that the other girls' conservatism would rub off on me.

It didn't work. I just didn't fit in.

I lasted one miserable year before I stopped going to classes altogether. At the time I figured this was the only way to get myself out of a place that I loathed. And it worked.

My parents allowed me to drop out and then sent me to England for two weeks. I think their logic was that if they sent me to my mother's birth country it would jolt my mind back to their normalcy. I had a wonderful time, but it didn't change who I was, or wanted to be.

When I returned from England, my parents and I came to a mutual agreement. I had to finish my schooling, but they agreed that I could pick the college. I was all for that and chose American University in Washington, DC, known for its excellent design curriculum. And it was also known for a very forward-thinking student body and staff. In two years, I earned my degree in design.

I realize now that I really was a hypocrite of sorts back then: accepting my parents' gifts, knowing that they hoped their generosity would guide me back to their accepted path. All the while, I knew it wouldn't. I remained determined to travel my own life's journey.

But there was one more decision I would make that would finally tip over the rocky boat that was my relationship with my parents.

Chapter 2

After graduation, I landed an entry-level job as a graphic designer for a local newspaper. With the promise of a steady income, I announced to my parents one Friday evening when I returned from work that I would be moving out of the house that weekend and renting an apartment with a coworker. "I've signed the lease and I'm leaving tomorrow," I told them.

As the words finished exiting my mouth, my mother announced, "You can't leave this weekend. You have a date with Charles on Saturday night. You remember me telling you about him, don't you? He's a midshipman at the Naval Academy and is staying with my friend Lois."

"No, Mom, I am not going on that date. All the Naval Academy guys you have set me up with before are pompous and very boring. You'll have to call Lois and tell her I can't make it," I stated firmly.

From the corner of the family room, while sitting in his leather recliner and reading his newspaper, my father joined the conversation. "You're going on that date, Mattie. There will be no further discussion. He's from a good family and has a great future ahead of him."

Still not ready to fully unfurl my independent wings with my parents, and especially with my dad, I agreed, even though I knew that it would not turn out well. Charles—or Chuck, as he was called by his friends, would tout up all his attributes, hoping that his selling points would give him the opportunity to get to first base.

It never worked before, and it didn't work that Saturday night.

I moved to my new apartment that Sunday.

What a wonderful and invigorating experience it was to live on my own. I felt completely free. Yet, to be honest, I was nervous, especially regarding all the bills that had to be paid. I had never, ever had to worry about paying bills. I had never had to pay for anything before.

About six months into my job, I agreed to go out to a local bar one Friday night with my girlfriend Cathy. We were having a great time talking and gossiping when Cathy nudged my hand and said, "I think that guy over there wants you to dance. But don't turn around, because he's heading our way. Be cool."

Just as I finished rolling my eyes at Cathy, I felt a presence next to me. When I looked up, ready to tell him I wasn't interested, I saw the face of a very handsome man sporting a military haircut and tight pullover shirt that accented his very buff arms. Another academy guy.

"Sorry, I don't date midshipmen."

"I'm not Navy; I'm a Marine, so you can at least agree to dance with me."

I was taken aback by his directness, yet a bit charmed, so I agreed to one dance.

That was the night that I met the man who I would dance with for the rest of my life.

I met David Hill.

He was from our hometown: a high school football hero and son of parents that owned a well-established real estate company in the area. He was everything my parents hated. He was not a lawyer, a doctor, a college graduate, or an established businessman. He was an enlisted man in the Marine Corps.

Somehow David made me feel like "Mattie" for the first time in my life, and I fell completely head over heels in love with him. He was my knight in shining armor, rescuing me from the traditionalist life my parents had wanted for me.

As our relationship grew, David introduced me to his parents. They were welcoming and supportive of us. Oddly enough, our fathers had met each other once before. They had met in Laos in the early '60s when they both were serving in the Army overseas.

Then, I introduced David to my parents. They were not happy.

During that initial meeting, my mother pulled me aside and said, "He's not up to your caliber, Mattie. He will let you down. You're probably just a fling to him." I didn't respond to my mom, as I watched my father scowling from his chair while David struggled to make polite conversation with him. My parents were certainly not polite or accepting that night.

"That did not go well," I said to David as he drove me back to my apartment.

"It's okay, Mattie. I got this. I may be enlisted, but I know how officers' minds work. My dad's an officer. How hard can it be to win your father over?"

"It's going to be an uphill battle," I answered. He walked me to my apartment door, and we kissed deeply. My heart exploded with love for him. As he turned away to leave, he said, "I have no idea what our future holds, but rest assured, I'll always take care of you, Mattie."

And I knew in that instant that he would.

Later that week my sister Carole called me and mirrored my parents' concerns, stating that "David will not be able to give you the life that you are used to. You were raised with the finer things in life. And eventually you'll become angry with him because you don't have those things or the opportunity to get those things."

I answered crisply, "Carole, the life that I have led up to this point is not the life I want to have. I don't want to sit around my dinner table judging people or condemning people because they don't dress a certain way or live in the 'right' community or attend the 'right' school. I want my dining room table filled with people of character from all walks of life, not just those that wear Lacoste shirts! And besides, David was raised with the finer things in life too. His father is a retired officer as well."

"Well, Mattie, I wish the best for you. It's not going to be an easy road, but always remember that I love you and I will always be here for you."

Remembering back, I always loved how my mom would set our table at dinnertime. And she did this every night. She would dress the table with a crisply starched Irish linen tablecloth, fresh flowers, silver candleholders with lit tapers, bone china, sterling silver utensils, and Waterford glasses. It was a lovely experience to dine at her table, and her hostess skills were the envy of the neighborhood, as well as her cooking skills. But in my heart, I wanted my life to be much more evolved than just table fineries.

One day, David secretly asked my roommate for the key to our apartment. And in the afternoon, while I was at work, he decorated the apartment with roses, and candles. When I walked into the apartment after work that evening, I was greeted by candlelight, soft music, and David on one knee in the foyer with an open ring box in his hand. He didn't have to ask me twice: I said yes. Like Rose in the movie *Titanic*, I had made my choice, and I chose David.

The next day, I went over to my parents' house so excited to show my mom the engagement ring on my finger. It was a flawless diamond set in 14-karat gold with baguettes on both sides. It wasn't a huge diamond, but it was perfect.

"Mom," I called out as I entered my former home. "Where are you? I have something to show you." I was so excited to show my mom. Perhaps when she saw the ring on my finger, she would realize that David and I really were serious about each other, and I wasn't "just a fling." Finding her in the kitchen, I rushed up to her and hugged her.

Pulling away from our embrace, I held out my left hand. "Look Mom, David and I are engaged. I am so very happy!" As I held my hand out in joy, my mother coldly looked at me and said, "Your father and I will never accept this marriage." Then, she left the kitchen.

It was then so brutally clear how I had been right about my parents all along, and it broke my heart. With my happy news shattered, I felt completely alone.

Life had just handed me my first challenge. I had lost the support of my family because of my decision to be with David, and now I would have to navigate life with just David.

However, that young Mattie did not give up. And I'm so glad she didn't. Because I knew that with David by my side, we could and would conquer everything life dished out to us together. Oddly enough, we did a pretty good job.

Chapter 3

David and I were married by a military minister in a little duplex that he'd purchased several months prior to our wedding. My mother and sister were present. David's parents and his brother were there. My father was glaringly not present. He refused to join in the celebration.

Within a year we found out we were expecting. Our first child was a girl, and we named her Claire. She was healthy but colicky and consequently a lot of work. More work than I had ever envisioned as a new mom. I didn't handle the situation or her well.

David would often come home from work to a baby screaming in her crib while I sat on the couch crying.

I would say to him almost daily, "I've tried everything, David. I've nursed her; her diapers are clean;

we've gone outside for some sunshine. I just don't know how to make her happy. I'm a failure as a mom."

He would calmly say, "No, you're not, Mattie. She's just fussy, and you're stressed. She senses that. Do you have some of your milk in a bottle?"

"I do."

"Warm up a bottle while I go get her."

I would bring the bottle to him, and as he sat in his recliner with Claire—who had instantly quieted in his arms, by the way—he would give her a bottle, still in his military cammies, while I watched, astonished, as my daughter peacefully enjoyed her bottle with her dad.

After several months of David being the go-to person with our firstborn, Claire and I got into a routine. Honestly, I finally relaxed in my new role. And boy, was I happy. I was thrilled to be a mom. I was on top of the world as Claire grew and flourished.

When Claire was about three, David asked if I would like to have another child.

"Absolutely. You want a boy, don't you?"

"Well, of course, I'd love to have a son. Don't get me wrong, Claire is wonderful. Even at this young age you can tell she's athletic, and I love hanging out with her. But I would love a boy to carry on my name."

"David, you don't have to ask me twice."

For two years we tried. And nothing. It got to the point where David even knew when my cycle was due.

"Have you gotten your period?" he would ask.

"Yes, it started yesterday," I would answer. I watched as his face fell into a mask, crestfallen that we hadn't conceived once again.

I wondered what was wrong. Claire came along so easily. What is so different now? I asked myself every month. I tried not to worry about it, but I did. I so wanted another baby.

Claire was almost four when finally my period was late.

Hallelujah!

When I told David, he danced around the living room.

"I just know it's a boy. I just know it! I'm so happy, Mattie."

I was happy too.

"Have you made an appointment with the OB?"

"Yup, it's next Tuesday. Do you want to come?" I asked.

"Absolutely," he replied.

I never told David this, but I was worried about this pregnancy because something just didn't feel right. I didn't feel the same as when I was expecting Claire. Every pregnancy is different, but I sensed that this pregnancy was not viable.

We went to the appointment the following week, and the doctor said everything looked good. I was about nine weeks along in the pregnancy.

A week later, I started cramping. By the time David got home that night, I was spotting.

"David, I'm bleeding." I cried.

"What?"

"I think I'm losing the baby."

"No, it'll be okay. Did you call the doctor?"

"Yes. He said to rest."

"Well, that's what you'll do. Just rest. Everything will be fine, Mattie."

I knew it wouldn't be. That sense that something was wrong was pinging off my radar.

David insisted on taking care of Claire and me. He would prepare Claire's lunches and send her off to school every day. He made me breakfast and would prepare lunch for me as well, all before he headed off to work. The only thing I had to do was rest and greet Claire when she returned from school.

The spotting continued.

One afternoon, before Claire came home, my back seized up with cramps that no menstrual period could touch. I got off the couch and gingerly walked to the bathroom. As I sat on the commode, I looked down between my legs and saw my one-and-a-half-inch baby floating in the toilet bowl. Our baby was almost three months old, and now it was gone. I had lost the baby.

Devastated, I called David's office. At the time he was a Marine Corps recruiter, so he was out on the road somewhere. I left a message with the Marine on duty that it was an emergency and I needed David to contact me immediately after he got back to the office. There were no cell phones at the time.

As I continued to hemorrhage, I knew I had to get to the hospital. I called my neighbor, and she said she would be right over to take me to the hospital. I then called another neighbor, explained what was happening, and asked her to come to the house to meet Claire when she got off the bus. She agreed.

As I was wheeled into the emergency room, I prayed for David to arrive. He didn't. They did a dilation and curettage, better known as a D&C, and admitted me overnight for observation.

Finally, around 7:00 p.m., David entered my room.

"Are you okay, Mattie?"

"No, David, I'm not. I lost our baby." I wept. "It was horrible. I saw our baby in the toilet. I'm so sorry."

"It's okay, Mattie. We'll have another one."

"What if I lose that baby too? I feel like I've failed," I said.

"You haven't failed. Just rest. I'll pick you up tomorrow. What time are you going to be discharged?"

"By 10:00 a.m.," I replied.

I couldn't help but notice that David was wiping away tears as he left my hospital room that night.

Honestly, I've never gotten over losing that baby. My child was literally expelled from my body and died. I had lost something that was so precious to David and me that I wondered if I could ever handle being pregnant again.

A week later, I went to my OB/GYN, and he told me everything looked fine. David was with me, and the doctor looked at both of us and said, "Mattie needs to heal. When a woman has a miscarriage, the uterus needs time to recover and be ready to nourish another fetus. Do not get pregnant again for six months."

It didn't seem unrealistic to us. It had taken us over three years to get pregnant after Claire, so we just nodded our heads in agreement.

Three months later, I was pregnant with Ethan.

When I went for my first prenatal checkup, my OB doctor just looked at us and said, "Really? I told you guys to wait. Because of Mattie's recent history, I'm going to designate Mattie and your baby as a high-risk pregnancy."

"Why?" David asked.

"Because when we did the D&C on Mattie, her bleeding was excessive. Because of this we analyzed the blood from her placenta and the fetus in case she didn't stop hemorrhaging. When the results came back, we noted that Mattie has a genetic irregularity that can lead to Down's syndrome. It is called Trisomy 21. There is a 10 percent chance that this baby will have Down's syndrome. I would recommend doing an amniocentesis, which is the process of pulling fluid from the uterus to see if the baby is viable. I must also warn you that sometimes this procedure can cause a miscarriage." Boy, let's add another factor to my list of feeling like a failure. But immediately I said, "No, I will not do that."

David looked at me and said, "Mattie, do you really want to chance having a special-needs child?"

"David, that's not the point. Only God has the right to determine our child's life. I will not jeopardize losing this baby just because of a 10 percent chance that he or she is not normal. The conversation is over."

David looked at the doc and said, "Mattie has spoken."

As the pregnancy continued, I knew, deep down, that this baby was a boy. Our baby flourished to the point that, at four months, my doctor wondered whether I was having twins. I was huge. I was scheduled for my first ultrasound the next week, and lo and behold, my instincts were correct. David and I were having a boy, and it wasn't twins. It was just a *big* baby boy.

Because I was high risk, I was seen on a weekly basis. And I prayed constantly.

"Please, God, don't let me lose this baby. Please don't let him have my weird chromosome. Please let him be normal."

It was my nightly prayer. I didn't want to let David down again.

At eight months, I had already gained forty pounds. Probably because David didn't let me do anything other than eat and sleep.

I was happy, though. I was going to give David the son he so wanted.

Our baby was due February 21, 1990. Two weeks prior to the date, I lost the mucus plug. This is one of the first signs that labor would begin soon. And then nothing. My water didn't break, and I had not a twinge of labor pains. Then, early on the morning of February 22, I woke up to massive labor pains that radiated from my back around to my belly.

"David, wake up. Ethan's coming." We had already named him. We both felt it was important to have a name for your baby before he or she arrived.

David hurriedly called a neighbor and dropped Claire off there as I sat in the van, breathing through the contractions.

Thankfully, we arrived just in time. But unfortunately, not in time for an epidural or any of those wonderful pain-blocking drugs.

After thirty-six hours of labor, our son was born early the next morning, perfectly healthy and a whopping eight pounds and fourteen ounces. I had done it. I had delivered a healthy son for David.

And wow, he was beautiful. When I held him, I felt such joy that it bubbled up from my very core and threatened to overflow, from the sheer satisfaction of being a mom again. I looked into his eyes, the same blue as mine, and I was in complete awe at this wonderful creation that God had granted us. He was part of me, and it touched my soul by the sheer wonder of him.

Welcome to the world, Ethan Benjamin Hill.

We left the hospital two days later, and it was evident from the start that Ethan and I were connected. He eagerly latched on and nursed as David and Claire sat idle, wondering what they should or could do to help me.

"Nothing," I said. "I got this."

The months and years flew by as Ethan grew into a stocky toddler and then a strapping young boy that loved baseball, tennis, and anything that went fast!

Claire continued to amaze us with her natural aptitude for school and her uncanny connection with animals. We had a menagerie: a dog, a cat, a rabbit, and a mouse, and she took care of them all. When she was about ten, she announced one night at dinner, "I think I would like a horse."

David and I looked at each other, aghast. A horse?

David spoke first. "Well, Claire, I don't think it would be logical to buy a horse right away. How about riding lessons?"

"Yes, that's what I want to do," she proclaimed.

A few weeks later, riding lessons for Claire were secured and worked into our schedule.

David and I were completely content. We were a young family navigating life. As I let those wonderful memories of my life as a young mother engulf me, I continued writing my story.

Chapter 4

David's military career brought us to the charming town of Beaufort, South Carolina. (Just so you know, it's pronounced "Buufort.") This little city is full of history and conveniently located near beaches, museums, good schools, and business opportunities. We ended up buying an older home, and we truly loved the charm of it; even if David was not a fan of all the upkeep. But it was perfect for our young family. Plus, we could afford it!

Our beautiful southern home was located on a shaded avenue, with a porch that surrounded the whole house. The windows on either side of the front door were transom windows that went from the floor to the ceiling. On pleasant days you could open them from inside and walk directly onto the veranda. It was built in the 1920s, and a swing complemented the wrap around porch. It stood on a lot that had one-hundred-year-old pecan trees and live oaks that dripped with Spanish moss. The backyard was filled with pockets of camellias and gardenias that filled it with a wonderful fragrance. Inside, there were three fireplaces surrounded by beautiful millwork and tiling. Unfortunately, none of the fireplaces worked. Our home had all its original floors, which glowed with a soft honey patina. Thankfully, the kitchen, the bathrooms, and all the inner workings of the house had been updated. And it had central air! That was a necessity in South Carolina.

Claire and Ethan had their lives filled with school and extracurricular activities, and as many parents do every day, we somehow juggled all their needs with our work schedules and other life obligations. We enjoyed it and loved the energy of our busy lives.

And I thrived as a mom. I had secured a management job in marketing, and even though I worked full time, I always seemed to have enough energy to meet my children's needs. I believe that was the period when I felt whole and completely satisfied with my life. I was needed by my children, by my husband, and by my counterparts at work. I was valued and respected.

Since Claire had several years under her belt riding horses, she began to compete in local shows. In fact, she and I spent many summer evenings after I got off work at the barn. Secretly, both David and I were thrilled with this, reasoning that it would keep her from exploring other pastimes that are every parent's nightmare. Claire was a quiet soul, yet very determined in excelling at any endeavor. She had her dad's competitive drive—which, between you and me, I was very envious of. Although I was very athletic, I did not have that competitive mental gene that she and her father were blessed with.

Ethan continued to be our free spirit. I recall that shortly after his birth, the OB nurse came in to tell me that she needed to take me to the nursery. Exhausted from the delivery and now totally stressed from not knowing what the issue was, they rolled me into the nursery in a wheelchair to find out that Ethan was completely unhinged because he couldn't roll over. One of the staff nurses gently consoled me and asked me to try and comfort Ethan. Well, I just picked him up and cradled him, and he fell instantly asleep. I just wondered why they hadn't picked him up…but never mind on that one. Perhaps they had, but Ethan needed me. At least that's what I like to think.

The head nurse—Nurse Jackie, if I recall correctly—informed me she had never seen any newborn so adamant about wanting to turn over and get off his back! Little did I know that this was a sign of the personality that would emerge: a person that would always vocalize his wants and desires in a very strong fashion. Where Claire was reserved, Ethan was an outgoing child, full of charisma and very opinionated. He, too, had loads of athleticism and intelligence. Unfortunately, he was reckless and carefree. And those traits would eventually play a huge role in our family's future.

That said, we continued along with our personal and family endeavors. David had retired from the military, and he had started a new business that was growing rapidly. The children were involved in school, sports, and other pastimes. We all were working toward our individual goals and somehow remained sane in the process. Probably because we had each other to lean on.

The years passed. Claire graduated from high school with honors and was enrolled at Virginia Tech, her dream school. She majored in veterinary medicine. To say we were proud of her is a gross understatement.

David and I knew that our lives would be changing soon. Claire was gone, and Ethan was a sophomore in high school, so we had begun discussing what we would do next. Personally, I was very happy to stay right where we were: at home in South Carolina. But David wasn't.

I vividly recall one particular night of our discussions.

We were sitting on the back deck that evening, surrounded by the sultry South Carolina spring air that was giving us a warning of what was to come in the upcoming months. The cicadas were very vocal in the moss-laden trees, and the gulls were squawking off in the distance, actively telling us that summer was right around the corner, or that there was a storm brewing off the coast.

Our discussion that night led to what the next step in our journey should be. Claire was in college and Ethan had only two years left in high school.

My husband always had great childhood memories of the family farm situated in the Deep South, where his parents currently lived. The property had been in his mother's family since before the Civil War, and he felt strongly about moving down there to assist his parents as they got older. I sure wasn't sold on the idea and told him so.

"David, I do not want to leave my home. You have a thriving business; I am now the director of marketing for a large company: Why in God's name do you want us to pull up stakes and go down there? There is nothing there except a big house and lots of woods! And Ethan hasn't finished high school. He's a sophomore. Do you really think pulling him out of his school to move there is the right idea?"

"Mattie, I'm the eldest male. My parents are getting old and living in that big house all by themselves. There is no one to take care of them or the property. It is my responsibility as their son. And, out of all their children, we can do it financially."

"I don't want to, David," I said firmly.

"Why not? I don't understand."

"David, I do not want to go down there. I won't have anything to do, and you're asking me to leave everything that I have known and loved for almost fifteen years. I just don't want to go. This is my home."

"Mattie, you really are not telling me any reason why. What are you afraid of? We have always loved to face new challenges. Why is this any different?"

"What am I afraid of? Everything. You are asking me to leave my bubble that I am in complete control of and one that I am very content to remain in," I thought angrily.

But instead, I said, "Because, David, I will be the one taking care of your parents while you are working on the property. I don't know anything about taking care of the elderly. What if I screw up? Your sister and brother will blame me because I am supposed to be the caregiver. And I am not a country girl or a southern girl. I don't know how to can anything or clean a deer or, heaven forbid, understand a Baptist preacher. This is not what I want to do. I know I won't fit in, and I am just plain scared."

"Mattie, I know you. You will always find something to keep you busy. Plus, you always make friends. Everybody loves you. Regarding my mom and dad, all you need to do is make sure that they have their pills and eat well and listen to their stories occasionally."

"Why don't we just hire someone to come in and look after Poppa and Mamaw?"

David said, "No, I don't want to do that. I need to be with them. Look, Mattie, I don't think we'll be down there more than five years, and then we can come back to South Carolina. Five years isn't that long, is it?"

"David, five years is five years, and I don't want to go." Fuming that he hadn't listened to me, I stood up, said good night, and went to bed.

The next morning, David apologized and suggested that we postpone the decision until Ethan had graduated from high school.

Hallelujah!

The next two years moved swiftly, and as Ethan graduated from high school, I actually found myself eager to leave my career 'dream' job. The company had recently been purchased, and the new corporate attitude certainly did not agree with my business ethics. It was cutthroat. The new CEO subtly made it clear that he did not want to keep me in the director's position. Taking his cues and knowing I couldn't win against the new corporate regime, I resigned. But I did make sure I received a year's pension. I had to have a little bit of control over the situation.

Since I was now without a job, and Ethan had graduated from high school, we agreed that it was now time to move down to David's parents' home.

I still had a lot of anxiety about this move—and by "a lot," I mean buckets and buckets of concerns. But I put my big-girl pants on and agreed to this new challenge. David sold his business, and we rented out our wonderful home in South Carolina. Our life in South Carolina was over.

Once we reached I-20 we headed due west, not in the least bit aware of how this new journey would affect all of our lives. And how it would change me forever.

Chapter 5

After a fourteen-hour journey, we arrived at David's family farm unscathed (thank you, Lord). David's parents greeted us with open and loving arms, as they always did. We unloaded our dogs, cat, suitcases, and boxes from our vehicles and began the process of moving into Mamaw's and Poppa's home. Mamaw and Poppa called it Magnolia Manor. And it was a manor. It was a huge home, over 8,000 square feet, situated on almost 500 acres of property that included fishing ponds, trails and hunting grounds.

Our household goods were not scheduled to arrive for at least another week. So, I spent a lot of time those first few days visiting with my in-laws. Spending time with them and seeing how their home was in disarray confirmed how much they really did need our assistance. They were not eating properly. The house was dirty, and flea infested. Their refrigerator was filled with outdated food, and the pantry was stocked with staples that had expired in the '90s. They weren't taking their medications as directed, and the property looked awful! Wow, welcome to my new challenge!

I knew they needed us there, and it was the right thing to do. But I really hoped I could handle this. It was a lot to ask of a woman that had already raised her children, had completed a successful career, and was looking forward to a peaceful retirement. But, once again, a challenge had been laid before me, and I was determined to step up and make the most of this new endeavor.

Truthfully, I kept questioning myself as to why I had agreed to this. I was really, really scared. Mamaw was a breast cancer survivor, and now she was in the mid-stages of dementia along with having type 2 diabetes. And Poppa had type 2 diabetes along with COPD!

I called Katie, David's sister, one day and bent her ear regarding my fears for over an hour. (I know, I should have called her before we moved, but I didn't. I trusted David and his choices for our family.)

"Katie, I am so afraid of this enormous responsibility of caring for your parents and all that it entails. I am petrified that I will fail. I'm scared that I won't get their meds right or watch Mamaw close enough, and her sugars will plummet, and she'll go into a diabetic shock. Can you please come down and help me for a while?"

"Mattie, the whole family has complete faith in you, but I am looking up flights down there as we speak. I think I can get down there sometime next week."

"Thank you so much. I really need you here, Katie, at least for a week or two so I can settle in properly."

Our moving truck arrived a week later, and as it navigated down the long, winding driveway leading to David's parents' home, everything seemed so very final. Once again, I wondered about the whole idea of coming here. Even though we had discussed everything as a family repeatedly, I couldn't stop worrying. What would this do to Ethan, pulling him away from everything he had known? What would this do to me, as it pulled me away from everything I had known? Could we survive this massive change in our family? I had expressed all my concerns to David more than once, and he always assured me that everything would be fine. But I was still worried. I felt completely out of my comfort zone. I was not in control.

As the furniture and boxes came into my in-laws' home, I tried not to be intrusive in unpacking our belongings and placing our furniture. I wanted to be respectful of Mamaw's home, so I asked her where she would like things to be stored or placed. But let me tell you, it was a bit overwhelming! I had her looking over my shoulder that whole day, questioning everything I tried to put away. And then Poppa would come in to give his opinion! Honestly, I don't do well with people overseeing me. I like to organize my things on my terms. "Just give it time," I thought. "You'll get into a routine; you'll adjust, like you always do, and everything will work out. And Katie will be here tomorrow."

Katie arrived the next afternoon. As she walked into the kitchen to see her parents, their faces erupted in delight. Mine did as well, because I knew my sister-in-law would offer me compassionate yet logical advice when we got the opportunity to visit one on one. Plus, I needed a woman to talk to.

About an hour later, Katie found me in the dining room unpacking dinnerware and glassware. She sat down on the floor next to me and started unwrapping items from the box I was unloading.

"So, how's it going Mattie?" she asked.

"So much better now that you're here, Katie. I really need a female companion right now. I feel so alone. David's always working outside, and I can only sit with your parents for so long. Don't get me wrong, I love their stories. But I have all this unpacking to do!"

"Why isn't David helping you?" She asked.

"He knows it's best to leave me alone during this sort of task. If he were here helping, he would try to tell me where to put things or ask why I had this piece of furniture placed here, et cetera, et cetera. It would not be good. He knows I like to organize by myself."

"So, you feel alone, but you don't want anybody here to help you?"

Giving her a side-eyed friendly scowl, I said, "Katie, it really irritates me how you can cut through anyone's bullshit and get right to the obvious point. You're a bullshit eradicator."

We collapsed in each other's arms, giggling until we were "snortling."

Katie stayed a full week, and in that time, she helped me tremendously, not only with the unpacking but also by lending an unjudgmental ear to my concerns. Our conversations sometimes led us to tears, but more often we found ourselves laughing uncontrollably as she would recount stories of her early years with her family, and I would share with her stories of my early years. It was a wonderful week.

When she left for the airport, we hugged deeply.

"Thank you so much, Katie. You have no idea how much you've helped me."

"I should be thanking you, Mattie. The whole family is beyond grateful for what you are doing for our parents. You call me anytime you need to. You got that?"

"I do. Thanks."

"And another thing: you are not my sister-in-law. You are my sister, and don't you ever forget it."

"Oh, Katie, I love you so much," I said tearily.

"I love you, Mattie. Remember what I said. Call me anytime."

As I watched Katie leave, I cried like I was saying goodbye to a best friend of many years. And I was. It's just that I had now finally realized it.

Within a month of Katie leaving, I had gotten all our belongings in place and had begun to settle into a routine. By then it was April, and I can still remember the muggy early-spring air filled with the thick fragrance of narcissus, jasmine, crocus, and daffodils that grew wild throughout the property. There are no words that can describe the sweet aroma that the combination of these flowers released, except that it is heaven sent. It made me want to just immerse myself in the blanket of aroma and lay in the blossoms, enjoying the splendor of the bouquet.

April at the manor became even more magnificent when the *Chionanthus virginicus* blossomed. It is more commonly known as a fringe tree and is a member of the olive family. A rather odd little fact, but it is something I learned googling the tree all those years ago.

The reason I brought it up is that the manor had this tree on the property. It was given as a gift to David's grandmother 40 years ago and now stood over fifty feet tall and was just as round. It stood majestically in the middle of the teardrop driveway in front of the manor. In my whole life, I have never experienced a scent as lovely as that of the fringe tree. Its aroma would float through the air and envelop you as you passed by its branches of blooms. The fragrance reminded me of a sweet, expensive French perfume. You know the one: the one-ounce Baccarat crystal bottle of perfume that was kept behind the counters of the highest-end department stores and cost close to five hundred dollars an ounce. To breathe in its scent was to breathe in the nectar of the gods. It was intoxicating. You just wanted to sit beneath the tree and let its fragrance wash over you. It was a southern ethereal experience. And when this tree bloomed, it signaled the arrival of the hummingbirds.

We aren't talking about five or six hummingbirds, as we commonly see around our mid-Atlantic feeders. We're talking about hundreds of hummingbirds. I recall how I would sit quietly on the back deck of the manor and let the multitudes of these magnificent creatures buzz, tweet, and dance around me. Their tongues would flick in and out faster than I could blink. Their magnificent feathers glowed and morphed in the sunlight. And then there would be that one bird, that gutsy one, that would come up to me as I sat, still and quiet, on the deck, and hover right in front of me chipping and flitting before it would rush off to the tree line. It was majestic and completely awe inspiring. It was the time that the Deep South was in all its glory.

To this day, I still love that memory.

The tree's blooming also meant that my horses would be arriving shortly to enjoy all this splendor. Claire was at the manor for spring break, and we were anxiously waiting to have them finally with us at our new home.

Chapter 6

In preparation for their arrival, David had been busy. He had been working the backhoe 24-7 for several weeks. He had evened out the pastures where there had been deep ravines that could snap a horse's or human's leg in a heartbeat—or a hoofbeat—into a smooth, gentle grade. While he was doing that, Ethan and I began removing all the hundred-year-old barbed wire fencing that surrounded the property. We inspected every tree in the pastures removing any barbs that were embedded in their trunks. Back in the day, David's ancestors had used the trees as posts to wrap the barb wire around to keep the livestock contained.

David had also hired contractors to build new pasture and paddock fencing and he had it painted a beautiful rich black. No white fencing down here. A white enclosure would not have survived the humidity here in the south, and within a year, every inch of fencing would have been coated in a green slime of mildew.

Thanks to David, everything was becoming equine friendly, and looking quite manor-like. Poppa and Mamaw were very impressed by the new curbside appeal of their property. One evening, Poppa told David that the new face-lift reminded him of what he used to see in the Virginia horse country. It really was looking quite beautiful, with the long, crushed-stone driveway lined by magnolia trees and the new three-board post-and-rail fencing surrounding the frontage road pastures.

David had also cleared all the growth around the front pond to the left of the driveway, so now there was a clear view from the main road across the pond to the new stables. I remember standing out on the road one day and looking through the pin oaks draped delicately with shawls of Spanish moss and thinking how stunning it all looked. It seemed to me as if the property had just jumped off the pages of a *Southern Living* edition, and I was in the middle of their photo shoot! Really gorgeous. God had created this beautiful masterpiece, and David had just put the final brush strokes on the canvas. I was proud of my husband and grateful for all his exacting labor.

In late May, our horses arrived. They eagerly escaped the horse trailer, happy to be able to stretch their legs and graze. On high alert, they snorted at their new surroundings and the smells of their new home. Both were Appaloosa geldings and had been a part of our family for many years. Yes, we had bought Claire her horses. (Well, we bought Claire a horse, and then David bought me a horse.)

Their names were Scotch and Whiskey. Scotch was a palomino Appaloosa, and Whiskey was a black Appaloosa. They both had beautiful blankets of spots on their hindquarters and were gentle horses with great personalities.

Scotch and Whiskey adjusted to their new home beautifully. There were acres of green pastures for them to graze upon, a pond to play in, and a beautiful stable to rest in. Honestly, taking care of the horses was a peaceful chore for me, as it gave me a reprieve from my other household duties.

Realizing I knew nothing about the care of horses except for proper feeding, I had purchased weeks earlier every book I could find about equine management and read them cover to cover. Prior to our four-legged family members' arrival, my barn was now equipped with everything needed to care for the horses. Bute, vet wrap, salt blocks, Wonder Dust, stethoscope, thermometer and Gatorade in case they didn't want to drink water, were all in place in the medicine cabinet, along with their deworming regimen. I had found a great farrier and vet and set up a schedule with them for my horses' hoof trimming and shots. Within a few months I was feeling comfortable handling this new responsibility. Realizing that we had a couple of extra stalls available in this beautiful barn that David had had built, I thought, "Why not start a horse-boarding business on the manor?"

I asked David what his thoughts were about this.

"I told you, Mattie."

"What did you tell me?"

"I told you that you always find something to do. Something to get involved with. I never had a doubt that you would find your place down here."

"Well, I'm not sure about finding my place, but it will give me something to do. And it would bring in a bit of revenue."

Within a month, I had my business license for my new endeavor: Magnolia Manor Stables.

I designed a logo and a flyer offering full board and trail riding and put them up around the various small towns nearby, hoping to get a few boarders.

Within three weeks, Magnolia Stables had two paying boarders! As the word continued to spread throughout the community, David and I soon realized that the next project should be a riding ring. David jumped on the idea and built a huge, fenced ring. He also built jump standards and brought in PVC poles for cavalletti exercises and jumps. Claire and I rode English, but none of my boarders did, so the jump standards and PVC poles were pushed to the outside of the ring, and the barrels and gaming poles came out to the center of the ring. David even built seating for spectators to watch as the southern cowgirls did their training with the barrels and poles.

Close to the end of that summer, I decided it was time to offer an additional revenue opportunity for Magnolia Manor Stables. The stables would provide lessons for beginner to intermediate riders in English or Western disciplines. Since Ethan was an accomplished rider, (particularly in Western) I knew I would have a backup instructor if I was busy with my other obligations around the house.

New flyers went up, promoting the new ring and horse lessons. Soon we were giving weekly lessons on our trustworthy Appaloosas. Our little endeavor then developed into a go-to place for birthday "horse" parties and trail rides. We had arrived and had been accepted in the southern horse world. It totally amazed this northern girl! And it felt very good to be validated as part of their world.

About six months later, I had a new boarder arrive, whose name was Beattie. She was into fox hunting. One day she asked me if I would be open to boarding some hunt mounts prior to their official state hunt.

"Of course," I said to her. "They just need to have their up-to-date Coggins, and the horses will need to be in the side pasture, away from my regular boarders."

And with that, I had a group of hunt folks coming on a yearly basis.

When they arrived, it was an especially thrilling time to witness at the stables. The riders would arrive with their huge horse rigs and their gorgeous thoroughbreds a day or two before the hunt. Sometimes I would ride in the ring with them as they warmed up their mounts. However, on my large pony, I did feel and look as if I were riding on a clunky, old four-cylinder Ford Pinto desperately trying to keep pace with their massive twelve-cylinder Lamborghinis!

As a thank you, they would often bring moonshine from Kentucky. Everyone would enjoy a sip or two in the evening once the horses were put out to pasture for the night.

I recall one evening we were all sitting under the gazebo, enjoying a sip of moonshine, when whispering started among my fox hunting friends. In a second, they all stood up and cheered Magnolia Stables as a fabulous stable, with gorgeous trails, pastures and riding ring, in addition to a hospitable host. "Oooorah," they shouted. We clinked our glasses of moonshine and toasted Magnolia Stables. Then another guest chimed in, "This property is beautiful. I rode out to the back pond this afternoon, and all the trails were clear, and the streams were easy to jump or ride through. Plus, we know our horses are well cared for. Beattie told me you and your husband have done all this in two years. Unbelievable."

"Well, it was a bit over two years. David did most of the work. But thank you for your very kind words. I appreciate it, and I will pass it on to David." If I were a peacock, my tail feathers would have been unfurling and twitching. I was proud of what we had accomplished.

I went to bed happy that night.

David never stopped working on the property. Whether it was clearing the never-ending undergrowth, building run-in sheds for the horses, expanding and installing fencing for the pastures, or removing years of debris from the trails, the property kept him busy ten hours a day. He was like a machine, and honestly, it petrified me that it would completely wear him out. And he was never in the house during the day. Yes, that was a bit of a 'bitch grumble.'

Thankfully my in-laws and I had settled into a workable routine. Their health had improved, mainly because their medications were now being administered properly and their diets were well balanced. However, I was having trouble keeping up with the housework due to the size of Magnolia Manor. I asked Poppa if I could hire some help with the cleaning, and he agreed. We were able to find a great gal who lived locally. Her name was Linda, and she was wonderful with Mamaw and Poppa, as well as a great housekeeper. With this new addition to the daily routine, I found myself with time on my hands, so I decided I would start up a small business out of the home in my field of expertise.

No small challenge, since at that time internet connectivity to the house was still dial-up. Other than dial-up, the only other option for internet connection at the manor was satellite, so that was the direction I went. Upon receipt of my business license, Magnolia Manor Graphics was up and running. After reaching out to prior clients and new ones in the surrounding area, what idle time I had was now filled with working with customers.

Looking back, I wonder whether creating all this bustle in my life was a way to feel in control. Or a way for me to survive. Who knows? A psychologist probably would have had a grand time analyzing me.

Two years passed, and one sunny spring day Claire was home from Virginia for a visit. She had graduated from Virginia Tech early and was now working on her doctorate in veterinary medicine. We happily caught up with each other's lives as we groomed the horses in preparation for a ride in the ring and then for a trail ride through the back forty (as the family called the back acreage).

About a half hour into our ride, Claire asked me, "Mom, are you okay?"

"I'm fine, Claire. Why do you ask?"

"You don't look happy. Mom, you look guarded, as if you're waiting for something awful to happen."

"Claire, I'm always on guard. I am constantly concerned about your grandparents' health and your father's health, since he works outside all day and every day. Plus, I'm running two businesses. My plate is full. There is no need to analyze me!"

In silence, we rode farther down the trail, until Claire finally said, "No, Mom, that's not it. You really aren't happy here. You need to tell Dad that you want to go home."

"Dammit, Claire, I can't do that. Everyone is relying on me. I really don't want to talk about it. I'm going back to the house." I turned Whiskey around and cantered back to the barn, knowing that Claire was right. She has always known how I truly felt. She was my firstborn and my baby girl. She knew me.

I had just finished putting Whiskey out in the pasture when Claire arrived back at the barn with Scotch.

"Mom, I'm sorry if I made you mad, but I'm worried about you," she said.

Hugging my precious, empathetic daughter, I answered, "Claire, don't worry about me. I have always enjoyed a challenge, and I have a big one now. I'll be okay."

Claire just looked at me, not believing a word that had come out of my mouth.

Neither did I.

Chapter 7

That summer, in August, the air was so heavy that even the insects had called it quits. And let me tell you, the insects down on the farm are truly from another world. Normally they don't go into hiding, but this year they were lying low, trying to survive the oppressive, cloying heat. There was not a croak, chirp, buzz, whir, or peep out of the multitudes that lived in this environment.

The heat had forced me to stall the horses during the day, turning on their individual stall fans and hoping it would provide them with some relief as the sweat dripped down their twitching withers and haunches and their heads hung low in disheartenment. They wanted to be out grazing, but as the temperatures hovered daily at 110 degrees with 99 percent humidity, I had to keep them stalled. I could only let them out at night. This was our fourth summer at the manor, and it was miserable, not only due to the temperatures but also to another curveball that life had thrown at us.

My mother-in-law had been diagnosed with stage IV cancer. She had beat it once, but it was now back with a vengeance. The insidious disease was in her bones and eating away at her bladder. As we attempted to travel gracefully through the next few months of caring for her, my life became filled with the daily routine of doctors' appointments, negotiating hospice care, hiring nurses, talking to medical personnel, and figuring out how to keep this gallant lady comfortable and dignified during the last weeks or months that she had here on earth.

Now, I must take a moment to tell you about this woman. My mother-in-law, Peg, was a force to be reckoned with. In her youth, she had left this very property and ended up in New York City. A talented dancer, Peg had become a dance instructor for Arthur Murray Studios. From there she'd relocated to Florida and taught dance in one of his studios in Sarasota. That is where she met Poppa.

Poppa, whose given name was Robert, had been a young officer completely enamored with the petite brunette and her gorgeous legs. He'd asked her to dance. And from that moment on they were an item.

I've just realized, as I write this part of the story down, that this is exactly how David and I met. He asked me to dance. Odd coincidence, isn't it? Anyway, on with the story.

After marrying, Mamaw and Poppa traversed their way through Poppa's military career, and upon his retirement from the military, Poppa decided to get his real estate license, and they commenced starting their own business.

Mamaw, never one to be idle, (sounds like me again, doesn't it?) became one of his agents and proceeded to become a million-dollar seller. Not an easy feat back in the '70s for a woman. She also dabbled in local politics and become the chamber of commerce president in their local town for several years.

Although a tiny woman, she was a mighty force to reckon with.

I remember all those years ago, when I first met her, she came out and hugged me. I stood rock still with my arms plastered against my sides, and as she pushed me back, she said in her soft southern drawl, "You truly are a northerner."

At that time, I felt like I had failed my first meeting with her. But then again, I had never learned how to hug spontaneously. My family weren't huggers.

So now, on to Mamaw's approaching final dance on this earth. When her desire to eat began to diminish, David and I began calling nearby family members to let them know that they needed to come and say good-bye. Over the following weeks, the grandchildren and great-grandchildren would visit and gather around her, speaking to her of their favorite memories. Mamaw would smile and nod at each family member as they reminisced. Often, I would sit discreetly in a corner of her bedroom with my camera and watch the interaction with her loved ones, ready to capture these precious end-of-life moments. Somehow, through God's grace and the autofocus of a digital camera, I was able to collect these moments. As I clicked away, I caught images of Mamaw as she held a grandchild's young hand in her heavily veined, liver-spotted one, or at other times I snapped photos of her as she rested her head against a great-grandchild to silently say goodbye. I was truly honored to be a witness to such a beautiful end to a well-lived life journey.

One of the last to arrive was Katie. Everyone was so happy to see her. Mamaw's face lit up when she saw her daughter. Poppa's shoulders seemed to relax by inches once Katie arrived. And I too, was ready to let Katie take over.

I watched respectfully as mother and daughter traveled through Mamaw's final days. Those last days were heartbreaking yet beautiful as Katie spoke to her mom about her memories and how much she loved their life together and what it meant to her. Witnessing this bond as they worked through it together cannot be described; it is not of this earth. It was a journey surrounded by memories of a lifetime sprinkled with bits of angel dust to soothe the tears that they both shed as Mamaw began her final passage. During this time, I still had my camera ready. Fortunately, before Mamaw said goodbye for the final time I was able to capture my favorite shot. Katie had leaned into her mom, and I snapped the image of the two women cheek to cheek, with Mamaw's hand holding her daughter's face.

Two days later, on a bright, sun-filled morning, while a brilliant, red cardinal sat on the sill outside her bedroom window, Mamaw died peacefully with her devoted husband and daughter by her side.

As we made all the necessary arrangements, Claire and other family members journeyed to the farm to honor the passing of their mother, grandmother, aunt, and friend. While folks gathered at the house, Poppa remained stalwart, befitting the retired army general that he was. When he kissed his bride goodbye as she lay in repose at the local church during her funeral service, there was not a dry eye among the many that had come to pay their respects. The pastor that gave her eulogy was one of my clients and spoke beautifully about how she was now dining at the Lord's table along with her other daughter that had passed before her. As he spoke those comforting words, Poppa remained completely upright at her coffin, determined to remain diligent in her memory. But for me and the other members in our family pew, there weren't enough tissues to stop the flow of tears. The emotions were overwhelming. When my sister-in-law, Katie, reached for me in her despair, I had nothing to offer except a crumpled, soggy tissue and my arm to hold her as just a small token of support for her and her family.

I loved Mamaw, and I respected her. Everyone mourned her passing.

Mamaw was buried in the cemetery next to the church that her ancestors built, right beside her other daughter. Her mother and father are one row over. All of them are under the shade of a massive pecan tree. A few weeks later, David and I found and purchased a stone bench adorned with hummingbirds and placed it underneath that tree to honor the special woman that Mamaw was in life.

Over the next few weeks, our family slowly began to adjust to the new normal of our lives without Mamaw. Poppa slowly accepted his new role as a widower. Yet he was so quiet. His wartime and business stories became less frequent, more than likely because he didn't have Mamaw as his dedicated audience. He grieved silently and alone. I felt hopeless watching him: a solitary man, no longer able to share his memories with his life-long dance partner.

Daily he would shuffle, unshaven and still in his nightclothes, to the kitchen for his breakfast. I would chatter away about mindless things as he gazed out the kitchen window, uttering a few comments here and there. I often wondered whether he was seeing in his mind's eye all his life's memories as he stared out that window. The memories of how he and Mamaw sold their business and moved south to care for her parents. How they imagined and then built their dream house, a house that was understated yet grand. A house that hosted weddings, Christmas and Thanksgiving feasts, church and military gatherings.

It dawned on me one morning as I sat with Poppa, that David and I had done the exact same thing. We had left everything we were familiar with. David had sold his business, I'd left my corporate job, and we'd left our home, neighbors, work, and community to come down to the American southland.

I asked Poppa one morning how he felt about all that he and Mamaw had given up coming down to his wife's family property, and he said, "I never wanted to come down here, but this property meant so much to Mamaw that I couldn't say no. I wanted to retire in Florida."

"Oh, Poppa, I know exactly what you mean. I never wanted to come down here, either, but it meant so much to David that you and Mamaw should stay here in your home as you got older that I couldn't say no. And I'm glad I did. Because no matter how hard it was for me to pull up my roots, I will never regret getting to know you and Mamaw better and that you allowed us to make your home our home. Thank you, Poppa."

"You're a good girl, Mattie. I need to tell you something. I have never thought of you as a daughter-in-law; you have been my daughter since the day I met you."

Trying not to let my emotions get the best of me, I hugged that old man as hard as I dared. His statement was so precious to me.

Somehow, we soldiered on, once again learning a new routine. This one was a routine that somehow felt off track to me, mainly because Mamaw was no longer with us. I never realized until she was gone how she had been the glue that held our world together. Her love for her husband, her son, and me had quietly grounded us all, and made us a family. Without her, we all floundered a bit.

But as the old idiom states; time marches on.

David continued the endless projects around the property, and for me, caring for one less elderly in-law allowed me to further expand my graphic design business.

Our kids had returned to their respective schools. Ethan had graduated from the local community college and was now enrolled at the state university located several hours north of us. Because of the school's proximity, he was able to come home more often for weekends. On one of his weekend visits during the fall after Mamaw passed, he brought his roommate Craig to go hunting and fishing with him on the property. During dinner on that Saturday night, Craig mentioned that Ethan was seeing a young woman who was also attending the same university. Of course, since Ethan hadn't said a thing about dating anyone, David and I were full of questions about this girl. Ethan gave Craig the evil eye for even mentioning it as I fired off all the normal parent questions.

"Where is she from? What's her name? What is she studying? How did you guys meet? When can we meet her?"

As Ethan continued to give Craig the voodoo eye for even bringing up his relationship with this girl, he unenthusiastically answered our questions, but barely. The basic information we found out was that her name was Megan, and she was a junior. She was studying English literature and hoped to eventually teach at the college level. Obviously, she had goals, which I found comforting. I hoped Megan would be a good influence on Ethan, supporting him in his school and career goals. We did find out that she was from a very Southern Baptist family, so her morals should be sound. So, with this new information about Ethan and perhaps a significant girlfriend, David and I were cautiously excited that he was in a good relationship that may develop into a lifelong commitment.

Pushing back from my desk, I review what I've written. Honestly, it warms my heart to remember the history of our family and the loved ones that were a part of my life at that time. It brings everything back to life. I can still smell the magnolias, and the fringe tree. I remember so many of the conversations around the breakfast table, not to mention the huge meals during the holidays! It also makes me realize that our family dynamic at that time was one of love, support, faith in one another, and caring about each other. Believe me as I say again, it wasn't easy, but we managed because we had each other's backs.

I get up from the desk and meander into the bedroom. Looking at my bottles of pills, thinking it's time to take one, it dawns on me that I don't want one! Wow, writing my story really is therapy. However, I do head to the kitchen and pour myself a glass of wine.

Even though it's late, I head back to the office with my wine. I want to write some more.

Chapter 8

College football was in full swing, and Ethan had finally invited us to come up and meet Megan. David and I asked Mark and Debbie, friends of ours and huge State fans, if they would like to come with us to the game. They happily agreed. Truthfully, my primary reason for wanting to go was to meet Megan, and I wanted a female companion as my backup.

Now, if you've never been to a Southeastern Conference college football game, you have missed the divine art of tailgating southern style. Students and parents alike stake their tailgating plots the night before, sometimes even a week before, especially if it is a rivalry game. In the early morning hours of game day, massive tents are erected, complete with widescreen TVs, smokers, barbecues, and large buffet tables filled with an abundance of all the football foods you could ever imagine: wings, fried chicken, subs, casseroles, smoked meats—oh, and I can't forget to mention full bars and kegs of beer! The aromas are sumptuous, and all the tailgating hosts are willing to share. Everyone is dressed in their respective school colors, with many sporting artfully painted faces, bodies, and other decorated body parts that I prefer not to mention. One of the traditions includes strolling among the tents and observing their displays of foods or their tent decoration, nodding in approval or clicking a tongue in distain, always behind a strategically placed hand or a turn of the head, so as not to offend anyone.

Preparing to leave for the game, David and I loaded up the cooler with our neighbor's famous fried chicken and potato salad, along with Mark and Debbie's ready-to-cook hamburgers and slaw. Another cooler held the normal tailgate liquids: beer, wine, and the ever-present sweet tea. Mark, Debbie, David, and I were scheduled to meet Ethan, Megan, and Ethan's friends at 11:00 a.m. to help finish setting up their tailgating area. When we arrived, Ethan greeted us, but Megan was nowhere to be found. I was disappointed that she was not there to welcome us, but I kept that to myself. Ethan explained that she was with her sorority sisters and would arrive shortly. Honestly, I felt rather rebuked, but David assured me it was no big deal. "Not according to you," I mumbled under my breath. My parents had raised me with exacting manners, and I knew that this was not the way a young lady should behave. For crying out loud, anyone brought up properly knows that you should always be there to greet your guests—and especially your new boyfriend's mother!

After an hour passed and there was still no sign of Megan, I really became irritated. Debbie, knowing me as well as she did, suggested we grab a drink and walk around the quad so I could vent—which I did!

"I don't get it," I said to Debbie. "If you are going to meet your boyfriend's parents for the first time, don't you think you should make an effort to be on time?" Debbie was in complete agreement but reminded me to focus on my behavior and not bring up my annoyance with Megan to anyone, especially Ethan. As we continued our walk among the crowds of football fans, chatting and visiting with other game patrons, I felt some of my concern regarding Megan's tardiness begin to ease, for which I was grateful.

We headed back to our tent about an hour later, and as we approached, both Debbie and I noticed a new visitor, a tall and willowy, blond-haired young woman standing next to Ethan. Could this be the tardy Megan? Nearing the group, Debbie looked at me and said, "Put your polite game face on, Mattie."

"Yeah, just give me a sec, Debbie. I'm still pissed off."

"I know you are. But just do it, okay?"

With my game face securely in place, Debbie and I approached our tailgating tent.

Ethan looked up and saw us, and he grabbed the young blond woman's hand and eagerly walked toward us. I added a warm smile to my expression as Ethan made the introductions.

"Mom, this is Megan. Megan, this is my mom, Mattie, and her friend Debbie."

"Hello, Megan, I am so glad to finally meet you. Ethan has told me so much about you."

"It's good to meet you both," Megan answered, then turned away. She found a chair, took a seat, pulled out her phone, and started texting.

Debbie and I gave each other the all-knowing look of mothers everywhere around the world: "What is wrong with this relationship?" We both wondered if she and

Ethan had had a fight, but Ethan carried on in oblivion, as if nothing was wrong, while Megan continued texting on her phone. And from that point onward, it was impossible to draw her into any form of conversation.

Immediately, this relationship did not feel right to me.

I pulled Debbie aside and said, "How rude can she be? I'm ready to go home, and now."

"Mattie don't be like that and stop worrying. Ethan seems happy. Let's enjoy the game."

And Ethan did seem happy. But since I'm a worrier by nature, I was not convinced at all. In retrospect, I wish I had listened to my inner voice and had enough guts to voice my concerns to Ethan.

We all went into the stadium to watch the game and sat in a row on the bleachers. I sat next to Megan, and every conversation opener I tried to engage in with her was met with a single-word response.

Well crap. This wasn't going well. And Ethan was three sheets to the wind after all the tailgating he had participated in. Perhaps that's why Megan was in an unsociable mood.

To add insult to injury, our team lost. Everyone helped tear down the tailgating area—except for

Megan. She sat in her chair, continuing to text. Ethan and Megan left without even saying goodbye.

"Great first meeting," I said out loud to anyone who could hear me.

Debbie, Mark, David, and I finished packing up the car and made our way home. I wasn't much of a conversationalist during the trip home. My mind was in an extreme state of concern for my son.

Chapter 9

Fall now had turned into a chilly, rain-soaked winter.

On occasion, Ethan would bring Megan home on weekend visits. Some of our weekends together had become quite enjoyable. We would play board games, shoot pool, or, when weather permitted, Ethan would take Megan out on a trail ride. One Saturday morning, they even went out hunting. As they headed out, I quietly laughed to myself at how out of place Megan looked in the camouflage clothing that she had borrowed from Ethan. It was not her normal go-to look. She was swamped in the overly large hunting wear but seemed eager to go with Ethan. It was during these times that I watched Megan slowly emerge from her shell. She seemed to be enjoying the new firsts in her life that she was experiencing down on the farm. "Perhaps I judged her too quickly," I thought.

In the spring of that year, Megan and Ethan visited less frequently, and when they did visit, Megan appeared sullen and withdrawn. I began worrying all over again.

I remember when I took the Myers Briggs Personality Test years before as part of training for work. My result indicated that I was INFJ. Basically, that means that I am introverted, intuitive, feeling, and judgmental. INFJ personalities are best known for their insightfulness. Essentially, that means that I am very good at assessing people and situations. Hence, I see and sense things that many others do not.

And I was seeing things that weren't right. What in the world was going on between the two of them?

I brought up my newest anxiety to David one evening over dinner.

"What do you think is going on between those two? Megan has looked miserable the last several visits. Do you think there is trouble in paradise? Maybe I should call Ethan to see if I can help."

David gave me a frown and said, "Mattie, would you please stop fretting over something you have no control over? You don't even know if anything's wrong. Leave them alone, for goodness' sake."

His comment didn't help. There was something going on with my son, and my 'mommy senses' were tingling off the charts.

One afternoon, while I was working on a project for a client, my cell phone rang. It was Ethan calling. I was on a tight deadline, so I didn't answer his call.

Within minutes my phone was ringing again. When I looked down from my computer to see that it was Ethan calling a second time, every molecule of my body went on high alert in a nanosecond. I just knew that something was wrong. Most mothers know that feeling, that innate instinct that your child needs you. When it hits us, we go through every scenario that could have happened to our child in a heartbeat. Were they in a car accident? Are they in jail? Are they hurt? Was there a terrible breakup? I answered his second call and calmly uttered, "Hello," hoping to disguise the fear in my heart as my chest hammered against my ribs waiting to hear the reason for his call.

"Hey, Mom," Ethan said cheerfully. Okay, he sounded happy, so this couldn't be too bad.

"Back at you, son. Are you okay?" I asked.

"I'm fine," he replied.

Well, thank you, Lord, as my heart slowed down from 120 beats it was beating in my chest to a mere 100. Yet, I was still on guard and very curious as to why he was so intent on speaking with me.

"Mom?"

"Yes, son?"

"Do you remember one of the things on your bucket list that you wrote down years ago?"

"Ethan, I have lots of things on my bucket list. What are you talking about? I have a deadline for a client. Is this a really important part of my bucket list?" I asked.

Now, just so you know, my bucket list contains a lot of silly things, like eating beef Wellington, riding a jump course in Ireland and winning, going to Wimbledon, (as a spectator only), and maybe getting a tattoo—so honestly, I was clueless as to why he was asking me this.

During the moment when Ethan asked me that question, my free hand rifled through a pile of notes on my desk, and I found my bucket list, laid it in front of me, and continued to work on my project.

"Well, this is the one that was at the top of your list," he said.

Even though I had found my bucket list, I hadn't glanced at it because I was focused on my project. In a second, I pulled one out of my hat as I continued to work and said, "So, you've won the lottery and you are going to take me to Wimbledon, right?"

"No, Mom. Wimbledon will have to wait. You're going to be a grandmother."

Immediately I reached for my bucket list. There at number one was "To kiss my grandchild."

What the frig!

I dropped to my knees from my office chair stunned, as I silently cursed my son for not listening to me about using protection. Yet in the same second, I was over-the-moon excited about a little one arriving, my first grandchild.

Now I understood.

This is the reason why Megan had been so out of sorts lately. No wonder. She was pregnant and scared.

Composing myself quickly, yet still kneeling on the floor with the phone cradled between my neck and chin, I asked, "How is Megan?"

"She's not doing too well," replied Ethan quietly. "She's petrified of telling her parents."

"But you told me," I said. "She can tell them."

Ethan's response was simple. "Mom, you and Dad are different from her parents. You always are there for me, no matter how badly I've screwed up. And, yeah, I've screwed up again. Her family is all about image and community standing. Her father is a deacon in their church, for crying out loud, and a local business owner. They will not handle this situation well."

I struggled to remain cool and collected as Ethan and I continued to talk. I asked all the questions: "Are you sure she's pregnant? How far along is she? How is she feeling?" He answered everything to the best of his ability. I then asked if Megan was with him, and he said she was. "May I speak with her?"

Honestly, this was not a conversation I ever expected or wanted to have with this young woman.

I heard a muted and rather tense conversation in the background. Then I heard the phone being handed over to Megan as Ethan said in the background, "It's okay. Talk to her." I gently said, "Hello." Megan answered me in a soft voice, and I knew instantly that she was ashamed.

"Megan," I said calmly. "Please know that I'm not angry about the situation, just surprised. I thought all young people in this day and age used some sort of protection."

Silence.

Shit Mattie, that was a stupid comment.

I tried again. "Megan, please listen to me. If you need to talk, call me. I'll take your call no matter what I'm doing. And know this. David and I will be here to support you, Ethan, and the baby with whatever you need. But I will say this: you must tell your parents and you need to find an OB doctor as soon as possible."

On the other end of the phone, I heard a muffled and teary "Okay," and then Ethan was back on the phone.

I had not put her mind at ease at all. She was a very unhappy and frightened young woman.

Upon hanging up with Ethan, I immediately went to find David to tell him the news. He was beyond ecstatic, just like Ethan. "Clueless males," I thought to myself. "You have no idea of what Megan is going through now, let alone what she will go through when she tells her parents. This little being is not part of Megan's life plan or her career track." I had a nagging sense of heartache in our future.

I told David my concerns.

"David, I just don't foresee a happy ending to this situation. I've never sensed a true commitment from

Megan to our son. She doesn't feel the same about him as he does for her."

"Mattie, you are just looking for something to worry about. Everything will be fine. You'll see."

I frowned at him, thinking, "Yeah, right!"

My sleep that night was fitful. I found myself twisted in the sheets and completely unsettled as David slept blissfully beside me. His mind was untroubled, while mine was filled with the worries of knowing that our son was about to travel a long and very rocky road.

The remainder of the week was filled with many calls to Ethan. He assured us that everything was okay, but Megan still had not told her parents about her pregnancy. This became a weekly routine, calling Ethan and checking in on Megan and whether she had spoken to her parents. The answer was always no.

David and I talked daily about this major development in our lives. On one occasion we reminisced about when we had found out that we were expecting Claire. Of course, it was a completely different set of circumstances, because we didn't have to hide it from anyone. We were married. We owned a home and although finances were tight, we were okay. And with that thought, I told him that I believed we should let Megan know that we would support her as a couple and as the baby's grandparents.

"David, we need to go up and visit Megan and Ethan face-to-face. It's been four weeks since we found out, and she still hasn't told her parents. I truly believe—no, I know—she needs someone to be there for her other than Ethan, because he's completely clueless regarding what she is going through." He didn't disagree at all with my request. I texted Ethan that we would like to visit that next weekend. He replied saying that would be fine. Our game plan was to reiterate our support and to urge Megan to speak with her parents. At this point, Megan was approximately twelve weeks along. Ethan and Megan had gone to the OB/GYN clinic, and they had found out the baby's due date was in late January.

When we arrived that Saturday just before lunchtime, Ethan and Megan were there to meet us. They had picked a restaurant where we could have a quiet, relaxed lunch—well as relaxed as it could be under the circumstances. As we sat pondering the menu, I couldn't help but see and feel Megan's misery. I saw it on her face; I saw it in her body language. Everything about her screamed "scared and sad." Ethan, being Ethan, was animated and talking about their plans for their baby. Megan's face showed none of the excitement. She was sullen, and even more disturbing, she was closed off to everything Ethan talked about. She sat in the corner of the booth as far away as she could from him and would snap at Ethan over any simple statement. Her body language and behavior told me she blamed my son for everything.

"Dear God, please help them through this," I thought to myself. "This is not a good situation."

When our food arrived, I was grateful for the reprieve from the awkward attempts at drawing Megan into conversations. I had tried my best to pull her out of her dark thoughts but with no success. Megan picked at her food, and Ethan kept pressing her to eat. Barely making eye contact with Ethan, she said, "I really don't feel like eating. This baby is a problem," she said and immediately fell quiet.

And with that statement, David and I just looked at each other with the silent communication of two people that have been married for many years, both realizing that she did not want this baby, nor was she committed to our son.

Ethan remained oblivious.

With nothing accomplished, and with our hearts heavy with the weight of this new knowledge, we left the restaurant and said our goodbyes. We were both solemn on the ride home, each of us aware that our son was in a life-altering situation that he was clueless about and both of us wondering what the outcome would be. Currently, it wasn't looking at all promising for any of us or our unborn grandchild.

As the next few days turned into another month, Megan still hadn't told her parents. She was now five months along. Oddly enough, there was a small blessing emerging in all this turmoil. Megan had suddenly begun to text me. She sent me her most recent sonogram, and then she began to call me after her doctor visits, updating me on how the pregnancy was progressing. With this small window of opportunity, I began sending her weekly inspirations with the hope that she would begin to see the beauty of the life that she carried within her and find the courage to talk to her parents.

I recalled a conversation she and I had after one of her doctors' visits. It was her six-month checkup, and she called me to let me know how everything went.

"Hey, Megan. How are you doing?

"Everything is okay. The baby is a bit small, so they've given me a diet plan."

I was sure the diet plan included more dairy, protein, and vegetables, none of which Megan cared for, except for cheese.

"Can I send you some money to help out with the groceries?" I asked.

"No, that's not necessary. I went and applied for WIC."

"Really? That's amazing that they approved you," I said.

"Well, I told them that I am a full-time college student with no income."

"Hmm," I thought. It's rather strange that Megan was perfectly okay working the system, just to avoid telling her parents that she was pregnant. I knew then that she was never going to tell her parents without someone being by her side. (How they didn't know already still baffles me to this day.)

"Well, again, if you need anything, just let me know. Megan, I have an idea. I would be happy to meet you at your parents' house one weekend so we can talk to your parents together. They need to know. Doesn't that sound like a good idea?"

Adamantly, she declined. "No, I don't want to do that."

The next week Ethan called me and stated that he wanted to ask Poppa if he could give Megan Mamaw's engagement ring.

"You'll have to ask Poppa," I replied curtly. Believe me, I really wanted to support Ethan in his decisions, but I knew with all my heart that this was not the right direction. Megan didn't want this baby or Ethan, and an engagement ring was not going to change that fact.

"Why don't you just tell her parents?" I exclaimed. "If you both would just be honest and tell her parents, you might be surprised. The worst they may do is disown her, and you know if that's the case, Megan would be welcome here." Ethan ignored my suggestion and was unyielding about the ring.

"No, I want to marry Megan. That's the right thing to do. I'll be home next weekend to ask Poppa."

I spoke with Poppa the minute I hung up with Ethan. I also let him know that I thought this was not the right thing to do. Poppa simply stated, "I'll listen to Ethan and make my decision."

The weekend arrived, and Ethan sat down with Poppa, as I sat within earshot in the other room. He spoke earnestly to his grandfather, stating that he hoped that the ring that had symbolized their love for over fifty years would again represent and solidify the young love that he had for Megan. Poppa asked Ethan if he respected her and really wanted to spend the rest of his life with her. Ethan said yes. Poppa then left the table, shuffled to the bedroom, and returned with Mamaw's ring. He handed the old leather box to Ethan and, shaking his hand, said, "I'm proud of you for stepping up and accepting your responsibilities. Remember, this responsibility is for a lifetime."

"Yes, Poppa, I understand."

I walked into the room, gave Poppa a hug and thanked him for his generosity and then left.

The negative vibes that I sensed about Megan and Ethan's relationship seemed to be mine and mine alone.

Ethan wanted to give Megan the ring at the farm. Even with all my concerns, I truly wanted to make this a memorable experience for them both, well for my son anyway. So, being the over-the-top, slightly domineering woman that I was (and am), I came up with a quick theme for the event. With Ethan's approval of my idea, we agreed to have the "proposal weekend" in two weeks. Working with the approved theme, I made a dog tag for Ethan's dog, Smokey, that said, "Will You Marry Me?" and gathered bouquets of wildflowers from the property to place them strategically around the various sitting areas in the garden. The plan was that Ethan and Megan would go and sit at Mamaw's special bench (she loved sitting there when she was alive) that was nestled beneath the live oaks, overlooking the front pond. Then Ethan would call for Smokey, and the faithful dog would obediently come to him.

Everything was going well on the day of the event, until Ethan called for his dog. Smokey, with his fancy collar and tag, had caught a delicious smell of something or other and decided he would follow that trail off in the wrong direction, so that plan failed. Ethan improvised, and as David, Claire and I watched from a discreet distance, we saw our son go down on one knee and ask this young woman for her hand in marriage. She accepted, and Ethan placed the ring on her finger. Honestly, it surprised the shit out of me that she accepted. I took the obligatory pictures of the happy couple and was informed immediately by Megan that I could not post them to social media.

Well, that didn't surprise me. Another red flag that nobody else saw.

A week later, I decided that the well-mannered thing to do was to send a note to Megan's parents regarding their engagement. I wrote a note, stating how excited David and I were regarding our children's engagement. And how we were looking forward to meeting them and their family while we planned for the union of our two children.

I believe Megan intercepted the letter because I never got a response. Yet, another red flag.

At this point, I had become crazy with worry, and I wanted this forced engagement to end. Those damn flags were blowing frantically in front of our faces, and no one else seemed to see them except for me!

I had to talk to Ethan ASAP and stop this craziness. Yet every time I attempted to have a conversation with him, whether sympathetically, aggressively or logically, he wouldn't budge an inch. He was confident that their love was real and assured me that everything was okay and asked me to please stop worrying and stop controlling his life. He was over the moon about this girl, and he truly believed she would stand by him.

During one of our conversations, my harshness came out, and I said, "Ethan, I know in my heart that she does not love you the way you love her. She will not stand by you."

"Mom, stop being such a bitch. You don't know anything about Megan. I do. She loves me, and we will raise our child together."

"I pray constantly that you're right. But I don't think so. You may want to listen to me on this one, son."

Ethan hung up on me.

I really hate being insightful sometimes.

Chapter 10

It was now close to Thanksgiving of that year, and Megan, of course, had yet to tell her parents that she was pregnant.

I remember saying to David one night, "I just don't know what to do. I need to do something. Should I call her parents behind her back? They need to know what is going on with their daughter! For crying out loud, the baby is due in two months. What parent cannot see that their daughter has gained weight and is withdrawn and wearing big shirts to hide her belly? And, for God's sake, what mother cannot see that her daughter is seven months pregnant?"

David did not agree and adamantly told me so. "Mattie do not overstep the current boundaries and call

Megan's family. Megan and Ethan need to step up and do the right thing."

"But David, they haven't done it yet. What makes you think they're going to do the right thing?"

"Mattie, I'm telling you to leave it alone. It is not your responsibility to tell them."

I just glared at him, poured myself a glass of wine, and went outside for some solitude.

I should have heeded my intuition, because neither of them stepped up.

Thanksgiving weekend arrived.

The minute Ethan pulled into the driveway the Wednesday before Thanksgiving, I attacked. I was beyond furious with him and Megan.

"How can you two be so irresponsible? There is a child at stake, your child and my grandchild, for heaven's sake! Fix this, Ethan, and now." He looked at me angrily and walked into the house without responding. Obviously, my son did not want to listen to my tirade.

We had over twenty people scheduled to join us for Thanksgiving that year. Somehow, I maintained normalcy, although my mind, heart, and soul were in complete turmoil. But this had been the standard for me over the last seven months, so why should this day be any different?

As casseroles simmered in the oven that morning, the kitchen was filled with the wonderful aromas that everyone instantly connects with during a family celebration. The potato casserole, green bean casserole, and stuffing were roasting in the oven, and the pecan and apple pies were cooling on the porch.

Sadly, all I could think about was my unborn grandchild and the drama that was sure to soon unfold.

David was smoking the turkey outside, enjoying his time with all the menfolk gathered around the smoker. I never understood this ritual of men standing around an outside cooking apparatus and discussing God knows what—perhaps it's a throwback to the caveman days, standing around a fire, grunting and scratching as they watched their recent kill simmer on the spit! Who knows? I sure didn't get it!

Anyway, since everything was under control in the kitchen and our guests were chatting amiably in the kitchen, I quickly removed myself, grabbed a sweater to ward off the autumn chill, and went downstairs to check on David's progress. Honestly, I really didn't care about the turkey, the casseroles, or anything else on this Thanksgiving Day. I needed to talk to my husband.

I had to make a stand.

Thankfully, in a few moments, I was able to pull David away from his man circle, and I strongly said to him, "David, I will not do this anymore. Ethan and Megan are not being honest. They have put us both in a horrible dilemma since they told us and not her parents. The situation has made us liars, and this has got to stop!" With that, David got really angry at me. "Why can't you leave this alone? You have got to stop trying to control everything. They are the ones that must grow up, be adults, and do the right thing. It's Thanksgiving Day, for God's sake, so would you please give it a rest? At least for today!"

I brusquely replied, "They still haven't done the right thing, have they David?" He didn't answer me, as he walked away to the circle of men.

I felt thoroughly chastised though, and on the verge of a major meltdown, I headed to the farthest bathroom from everyone and just sat my ass on the commode and sobbed. After several minutes, I was able to gather my composure, but just barely. I got up to wash my face, intent on removing any remnants of my recent crying jag and glanced in the mirror. What I saw was a middle-aged woman that I did not recognize—nor did I want to know her. It was not me. It wasn't Mattie, the happy young girl with light in her eyes, ready to take on the world's challenges. The Mattie I saw was weak, no longer in control of anything, and unable to protect her son from what was coming his way.

"Damn it all, stop dwelling on that woman's reflection and get yourself together. You're hosting Thanksgiving dinner, so put your big-girl panties on and get back upstairs," I said aloud to the reflection.

Plastering a fake smile on my face, I trudged up the stairs and resumed my hostess duties and visited with our family and guests.

All the guests had now arrived for our Thanksgiving feast. Hors d'oeuvres were served, and drinks and conversations flowed freely. Among the chatter of our family and friends, I heard Ethan's phone ring. As he answered his phone, his face said it all. It was Megan, and I knew in that instant, watching my son's face, that her parents now knew she was expecting. He quickly tried to get somewhere private to speak with her, but I heard the beginnings of the conversation as he scurried away from our guests, him clearly trying to console Megan, who was beside herself, sobbing and grief stricken. This was not good. My heart was breaking for them, for us, and for our innocent grandchild.

Thankfully, no one else noticed.

I quickly rushed to the kitchen to busy myself, and to—oh yeah—finish the final preparations for our dinner! My hands and my conversations with our guests were automatic as I handled my tasks, but my thoughts were a whirlwind of questions. "What did her parents say to her? Are they angry with her? Angry with Ethan or angry with us? Do they know that we have known about the pregnancy from the beginning?"

I knew it was Thanksgiving Day, and I knew I was supposed to be thankful, but I wasn't.

About ten minutes later, David brought the turkey up from the smoker, and as soon as I got the chance, I pulled him aside so I could tell him that Megan's parents had found out she was pregnant. I stood quietly next to him while he carved the turkey (which smelled divine, by the way); he asked me questions that I unfortunately could not answer. As he finished carving, he glanced at me and, knowing that we had to put on our best game faces even though our thoughts were elsewhere, took the turkey to the dinner table.

Poppa called everyone to dinner. Ethan did not come upstairs.

We all sat down at the dining room table, minus Ethan, and with heads bowed, we prepared for Poppa to say grace. As I held David's hand on my left and Claire's on my right, I glanced across the table from me at the glaringly empty chair where my son should be sitting. Gratefully, no one said a thing.

Poppa began his Thanksgiving grace, acknowledging all his family and friends around the table and what they meant to him, and just as he was about to finish and say amen, Ethan quietly slid into his chair.

Poppa, never one to finish a prayer quickly and always quick with his words, glanced at Ethan and proceeded to add to his grace the simple phrase: "And finally, Lord, look after my family and loved ones that I hold so dear this Thanksgiving Day. Please know that we love each and every one seated at this table with unconditional love, no matter what challenges life has dealt them, and that will never change. Amen."

I glanced at Ethan's bowed head and watched as he tried to surreptitiously wipe an errant tear from his face. His world was in chaos, and my heart and soul mirrored his unrest. I lifted up my own passionate prayer that everything would be okay for my son, for Megan, and for their child; my grandchild.

Dinner progressed without any more earth-shattering news, and once everything was cleared and put away and goodbyes were said, David and I had a moment to sit quietly and talk.

"What do you think is going to happen now?" I asked David.

"I have no idea, and I really have no idea how to help Ethan," he replied.

"I don't either. I called for him through his bedroom door after everyone left and he just told me to leave him alone. David, I am so worried about him, and just everything," I said, as tears threatened.

David reached over and grabbed my hand. "I know. So am I."

"Well, why in the world didn't you listen to me to begin with?" I thought. I knew I shouldn't have thought that, but I couldn't help but wonder if things would have been different if I had just acted on my intuition.

As the holiday weekend progressed, Ethan finally began to talk. And when he started talking, he didn't stop. We found out more and more about the downhill slide of their relationship, which didn't surprise me at all. Megan now barely responded to Ethan's texts or phone calls, and it was clear after our conversations with Ethan that she had not even told her parents that Ethan had proposed to her. So, obviously, the family ring that she accepted was never worn or shown to her parents (which I already surmised months ago.)

The fact that she had no respect for our family ring really wounded me and put a very sour taste in my mouth about this young woman. I know the situation was not ideal, but she had accepted the ring, for God's sake. The fact that she did not have enough deference to honor a lovely diamond ring set in platinum that was part of Ethan's family for over fifty years really pissed me off. Should I have been surprised? No, I shouldn't have, because this young woman was caught in such a turmoil that she had no strength to stand up for herself or, even worse, her unborn child.

All criticism aside, I truly understood she was a scared young woman floundering in a life situation that she had no control over. However, she didn't realize or understand—or care, probably—that David, Ethan, and I were suffering as well. And that we were just as scared as she was.

Chapter 11

After Thanksgiving, Ethan went back to school, and David and I resumed our daily duties. I continued to send out my weekly support texts to Megan, but now there was no response. My phone was silent.

I fell to me knees nightly and prayed—no, I implored: "Jesus, how am I supposed to deal with this shit?" (Yes, that is what I said, because that is what I felt. But I did apologize for the cuss word during my prayers!) "Please grant me the words or the grace to somehow reach this young girl and help her. This is an absolute freaking disaster! Our lives are falling apart, and I need your help!"

I never got an answer, and I was angry at His silence.

My mind continued to tumble about with thoughts about the unknown, but I managed to continue with my daily obligations. Whether it was feeding the horses, working for clients, or in the kitchen, I performed my duties without fail. But honestly, my mind was never 100 percent on task. Most of the time, I continued to fervently pray for a solution. But I still didn't hear anything from the man upstairs. It seemed He still wasn't ready to give me an answer. Consequently, I remained angry, scared, and a complete nervous wreck.

It was several weeks later that we received a text from Ethan that Megan's parents wanted to meet with David and me. We were both totally surprised at their request and very curious as to why they suddenly wanted to communicate with us.

Prior to agreeing to the meeting, David and I discussed that we should meet in a neutral location halfway between each other's homes. I looked up a suitable nondescript hotel halfway between each of our homes and texted Ethan that this was the location for our meeting. Within moments Ethan texted back that the meeting location was acceptable to Megan's family and included the time we should meet.

David and I had no idea what to expect from this summons, and unfortunately Ethan was not able to give us any clue, so we prepared for every scenario. The one thing we all were adamant about was that this child, our grandchild, would not be put up for adoption.

We would not waver on this point.

With that in mind, David and I came up with a very viable solution, or so we thought. We would suggest that David and I be the guardians of the baby once he or she arrives. This way, Ethan and Megan could finish their schooling and then decide how they would parent or coparent their child. It made sense to David and me, and when we mentioned this idea to Ethan, he readily agreed that it was a sensible solution.

So, with our plan in place, we anxiously waited for the appointed meeting day. And before we knew it, the day arrived and we were preparing for our meeting with Megan and her parents.

As I pulled clothing from my closet for our meeting, I knew that no deodorant could quell the eruption of sweat and anxiety that poured off me. I tried to dress appropriately, but all I ended up with was sweat-stained shirts and blazers, which I threw to the floor in disgust. I never imagined that I would be a participant in such a situation. It was beyond anything I had ever envisioned for my life. Finally, I just pulled on a comfortable pair of linen pants and shirt and brought a light jacket just in case. At the last minute, I put in my diamond studs and my diamond bracelet for a little glam. I wanted to show Megan's parents that although they thought I was just a glorified country farm wife, I knew how to present myself.

Before we left, I again got down on my knees and prayed that God's will would be done and that I would be able to be at peace with whatever His decision would be. Honestly, that scared me a lot: to pray for something that I had no control over was not in my wheelhouse, but I did it anyhow. I hoped it would turn out in our favor.

We were scheduled to meet Ethan ahead of time so we could get our game plan prepared. David seemed cool and collected. That was normal. But not me! My body continued to expel rivers of sweat, and I couldn't control my fidgeting. I constantly clenched and unclenched my fists, trying to relieve the stress. I found sitting in the car unbearable and shifted from side to side, hopelessly trying to slow my breathing as I watched the miles of highway go by. I was in a constant state of agitation. And, why in the hell did I wear linen to this meeting! I had sweat stains from my armpits down to my waist.

During the car trip, I talked to God constantly. I asked for grace: grace to listen patiently to the conversation that would occur; grace to find the words that would express our concerns without offending anyone during the meeting. I prayed for the Holy Spirit to guide all of us to a solution that was best for our grandchild and their grandchild.

David did not acknowledge my agitation, which was probably a very good thing. He was dealing with it in his own way. I had to respect that.

The silence was killing me, though.

Finally, I couldn't hold it in any longer. "Are these people going to yell at us? Are they going to blame Ethan for everything? What is going to happen to our grandchild? Dammit, David, why is this happening?" David was silent for much longer than usual. "Did you hear me, David? What the fuck is going to happen with our grandchild, and why in the hell are we having to go through this?"

He finally relaxed his grip on the steering wheel and replied, "I have no idea why we are going through this, Mattie, but we have been through much worse and survived. We have a family based on love and support, and that is why we are here right now in this situation, because Ethan needs us to be there with him, to show our love and support. You are killing yourself about the what-ifs. We can't control any of that. We can't control Megan or her parents' thoughts or decisions. We can only control us: you and I, and what we believe in and stand for."

David was completely correct in his assessment of the situation. But even though I heard his logic, I couldn't accept it, because it did nothing to soothe me.

We arrived at the designated location before Megan's parents. Ethan arrived shortly after, and we took the time to set up a seating arrangement away from others so we could have a private discussion. I really wanted a glass of wine; actually, I wanted to drink a whole bottle before I had to deal with them. But I curbed my Irish heritage and just opted for a steaming cup of hot tea.

We had just finished arranging the seating area when Ethan abruptly looked up. I glanced in the direction he was looking, and through the hotel window I saw Megan and her family exiting from their car. Looking at Megan, I saw a completely worn-out young woman. She looked awful. She seemed to have withered into nothingness, hiding behind her parents: sad, dejected, and overwhelmed by the decisions that she must face. I truly felt her anguish. I, too, was in pain. We all were.

Turning my gaze to Megan's parents, I saw two impeccably dressed people. Her father had on crisply pressed khakis and a button-down dress shirt along with spit-shined tasseled loafers. Megan's mother reminded me of myself before I refused to conform to my parent's traditional lifestyle: she had beautifully highlighted hair pulled back in a clip that enhanced her impeccably applied makeup. She wore a smart-looking shirt tucked softly into cute white jeans that accented her figure, and on her feet she, too, wore loafers. From my quick glance at her shoes, they were probably Hermès. Even from that distance I could see David Yurman earrings adorning her ears and a single Yurman bracelet on her left arm. I knew instantly that all their friends and associates looked just like they did. Molds from the most current catalog depicting what success looked like.

I glanced down at my linen sweat-stained outfit and my barn-worn hands and thought "Boy, do I look like a plain Jane! I sure didn't make the right choice on my clothing." But then I thought to myself, "Clothing does not make the person."

"There a nice-looking couple, aren't they?" I whispered to David.

"Yeah, they are. I think we may have a fight on our hands."

Before I could ask David what he meant, Megan's family entered our "meeting area," and we all surreptitiously sized each other up. We shook hands and watched as Ethan walked over to Megan and gently hugged her.

Megan did not respond to his hug.

Glancing over at Megan's mother, with her face rigidly set in disgust, I decided right then and there that I would behave in a more loving manner.

Walking directly to Megan, I embraced her fiercely and handed her the small gift that I had for her. As I hugged Megan, she hugged me back, holding me tighter than I expected. In that moment, I happened to look over Megan's shoulder at her mother. She stood there glaring at me with that same look of distaste plastered on her face, as if I were the she-devil from hell that spawned the boy-devil that impregnated her daughter.

Challenge accepted. I glared right back at her.

I hoped my gaze conveyed everything that I was thinking at that moment: "I'll hug Megan for as long as she wants me to. She is carrying my grandchild, and I knew long before you did, because Megan knew I wouldn't judge her or Ethan. From the time I found out, both David and I have been there and supported them both for the last eight months. And you didn't even notice she was pregnant until several weeks ago." I know it was bitchy of me to think it, but at least I didn't say it out loud.

Obviously, my prayer for grace had fallen on deaf ears. But hey, I won the first mom contest, because she broke eye contact with me first.

Pulling back from Megan, I said, "It's so good to see you again, Megan. I hope you like your little 'happy present.' Go ahead and open it now if you wish."

Megan glanced at her parents, and as her father slightly nodded, she opened her gift. It was a framed photo of her favorite dog along with a poem.

"Thank you, Mattie. I love it," she said softly.

Another point for me!

As we seated ourselves around the coffee table in that nameless, cold hotel, her family on one side of the table and ours on the other, it seemed as if we were all waiting for a chess match to begin. Who was going to make the first move, and what would be the countermove?

Megan's father played the first move, asking for us all to pray over this situation. Both Ethan and I tensed up, and David was astute enough to keep us peaceful, with just a look at both of us. Her father prayed for a solution to the situation, and one that both families would agree on.

He didn't pray for the baby, their grandchild, or our grandchild. He didn't pray for Ethan and Megan. I knew then that this meeting was not going to have an agreeable outcome. None of us said amen.

David, bless his heart, jumped in after Megan's father ended his prayer and added, "We should also pray for our children and their unborn child. This is a very difficult journey for both of them. And they need guidance and love. Don't you agree?"

Ethan and I loudly said, "Amen." Score three for our family!

David continued by eloquently stating, "With the upcoming birth of our grandchild, Mattie and I believe we have a valid and logical solution. We are not requesting to adopt the baby, but we are offering to be guardians of the baby after its birth. This way Megan and Ethan will both have the opportunity to figure out where their relationship is going, as well as allow them to finish their schooling. Once they are settled, they can then figure out what would be best for their child."

Silently, I applauded him for his quick delivery of the solution and thought there shouldn't be any reason that Megan's parents wouldn't agree to this option.

Well, Megan's mother piped in.

She swiftly moved forward in her chair and, looking directly at me, aggressively asked, "So who do you think is going to pay for this child?"

Megan visibly melted into her chair after her mother's statement. Her father gave his wife a side-eyed glare. I thought, "Oh my God, she's worried about money. What a bitch." I felt myself begin to boil with hatred for this woman, and thankfully David sensed that I was ready to pounce and placed a calming hand on my knee.

In seconds, I was in complete control, and as I looked over at Megan's mother, a.k.a. the bitch, I responded calmly, "Money is not an issue. We will gladly do this until the kids are settled and on a good path. Our grandchild's well-being is what is most important. Don't you agree?"

That silenced her for just a few moments, but then they threw us a massive curveball.

Megan's father leaned forward in his chair and said, "We have prayed about this as a family, and we think this is the right decision. We have found a good Christian home that will adopt the baby. It will be a private adoption, so no one will know. The baby will be loved and brought up in a church environment."

David and I physically recoiled from this statement. "What the hell are they thinking?" I thought. "Megan's mother was just asking about who would support the child monetarily, and now they are talking about a private adoption in a Christian environment?" How could they flip from money to Christianity in two seconds? It sure didn't sound Christian to any of us.

David, Ethan, and I simultaneously moved forward in our chairs and spoke strongly and in unison. "Absolutely not."

Megan hung her head in despair. Ethan clenched his fists, and his eyes were shooting daggers at everyone in his line of vision. I knew if we didn't put an end to this "meeting," Ethan would lose his composure. In those seconds, watching all this unfold, I felt myself begin to tear up, and I prayed that I would have the strength not to cry in front of them. I couldn't bear to let them see how much they had hurt us with this latest announcement.

Basically, they were saying that we were not Christian enough or acceptable to raise our own grandchild.

Megan had yet to say one word. Pretty sad that a mother-to-be would not voice her opinion about the child she was carrying.

With our unanimous rebuttal vocalized, Megan and her parents gathered their things, stood up, and left the room. Megan sullenly followed her parents out of the hotel. So much for prayers of grace—on their end, anyway. Personally, I thought we had all done a pretty good job of being graceful.

After we watched them leave, Ethan stood up and began aggressively shoving furniture around the room. We knew he was trying to get rid of his anger, which was completely understandable. Thankfully, there was no one other than David and me to witness his meltdown. However, we were both too exhausted from what had just occurred and sat in absolute numbness as we watched our son realize his life had just taken a significant nosedive.

One thing was certain about this meeting. Megan's family was urgently trying to protect their reputation and status in their community. They wanted no one to know that their daughter was carrying an illegitimate child.

That next week, Megan gave Ethan back the family engagement ring.

I have to stop writing. I've been writing day after day for weeks. I am exhausted putting all these memories to paper. And today was awful. Reliving all that anguish from years ago has made me angry and sad all over again. Glancing at the clock on my desktop, I realize I've been writing for over seven hours just today. No wonder I'm tired! My wineglass is empty, but I don't even consider refilling it. I save my document and leave my office. Placing my empty glass in the kitchen sink, I grab a tall glass of water instead of my normal refill of wine and think, "Wow, that's unusual for me. Water instead of wine—who would have guessed?"

Entering my bedroom, with my water in hand, I glance at my bedside table, at the bottles of pills waiting for me. I push all the "heavy" drugs aside and reach for the essentials...the blood pressure and cholesterol pills, a probiotic, and an aspirin. I don't want or need any of those other pharmaceuticals; I am just beyond tired.

Taking my pills with a sip of water, I lie down in bed, hoping to fall asleep. And, just like that, I fall asleep. And stay asleep.

I wake up hours later, and I'm amazed to see that the sun is just rising. Did I somehow sleep through the night? Glancing at the clock, I see that it's just after 6:00 a.m.

Oh my God, I slept seven hours straight. What a miracle! I reasoned it had to be the writing of my story. Somehow, putting the words down on paper and getting them out of my head really has begun to give me some semblance of peace.

Hopping out of bed, I head to the kitchen, prepare the coffee maker, and wait for a well-deserved shot of caffeine.

With a full, steaming cup, I head back to my office. It's a new day, and it's time to write again. I really don't want to go back and finish where I left off the night before. But I'm writing my story, and I need to write the whole story down, don't I?

Chapter 12

We rode home in silence after the meeting at the hotel. All of us were preoccupied with our own thoughts and concerns about the future. Another unsuccessful meeting with Megan and now a very disturbing gathering with her family was in the books.

As I pondered over all that was said, I knew deep in my heart that David and I had offered a great solution for both the kids. They would have been able to get back on track with their schooling and maybe even their relationship. With those areas settled, they could then focus on how to raise their child together. We were trying to be honest about the situation and looking for a solution that would be best for the baby and the parents. Our family wasn't worried about our reputation or the money because we hadn't hidden the situation from anyone.

Life happens. Deal with it.

I remembered that Megan had stated months earlier that the baby was "a problem." Our family had never considered that baby, our grandchild, a problem. That little being growing in Megan's womb was a gift. A beautiful, innocent gift from God.

It was completely beyond my comprehension that Megan and her family refused to accept this because of what it would do to their reputation. In fact, it really pissed me off.

Upon arriving home, David and I filled Poppa in on what had transpired. Even Poppa was outraged at their behavior. "They probably wanted to feel you both out about financial support. And even though you both acknowledged that you would support the baby, Megan's parents figured that they would get more money through a private adoption and their reputation would remain untarnished," he said. David and I looked at each other in complete astonishment. We hadn't even thought of that. Poppa's statement sure cut through to their real agenda.

Lying down in bed that night, I was so filled with anger and hurt over the direction that our encounter had taken that I couldn't fall asleep, thinking about the un-Christian behavior that we had witnessed just hours before.

After spending hours dwelling on everything, I knew I would never be the same person that I was before all this began. My heart had never or probably wouldn't ever again be so severely damaged by another person or family for the rest of my existence on this earth. And to my very weary mind, it seemed as if it were intentionally directed toward me. I know, that's a bit over the top, but that was how I felt that night.

Eventually I fell asleep. Yet after a few hours, I woke up abruptly, reliving the previous day's events. I untangled myself from the sheets and glanced at the nightstand clock, noticing it was only 3:00 a.m. Knowing that I wouldn't be able to fall back asleep, I headed for the kitchen to make some tea. As I waited for the kettle to boil, I wandered out onto the back deck. Looking up at the beautiful southern country night sky, I found some comfort gazing at the multitude of stars that seemed to be stacked on each other, layer upon layer.

As I continued to ponder the beautiful night sky, I began to see more and more layers, and it soon felt as if the stars were cascading around me, enveloping me in their warmth and glow. I stood peacefully, relishing the evening sky's beautiful blanket, and thanked God for giving me this opportunity to look past the bleakness of our current situation and witness His artistry. I hoped that the glow and light of His starry canvas would somehow bring light back into my life. I certainly needed it after the previous day and all its ugliness. We all needed His warmth.

Cradling my tea, I headed inside to the family room and turned on the TV. I found *Law & Order* and settled on the sofa, hoping that watching it would quiet my mind. I had been doing that a lot over the last several months, watching *Law & Order* and hoping for sleep. I sipped some tea and eventually nodded off.

The next morning dawned and, of course, nothing had changed. The unknown of our grandchild's future continued to loom large before us. Yet we all went about our daily routines. David was back out on the acreage working, Ethan was at school, and I was working on my clients' projects. But nothing felt normal or right.

Megan's due date drew nearer, and she had yet to accept any of my calls or texts since our meeting with her parents. Somehow, I managed to get through each day, but just barely. I prayed every night for some direction, some sign as to what I should do to help her and Ethan. I hated sitting idle, waiting for the unknown.

And then He answered my prayers.

Chapter 13

Two weeks later, on a Wednesday afternoon, Megan broke her silence and sent me a text. In her text, she asked if David and I would adopt the baby! I dropped my phone in astonishment. Picking it back up and re-reading her text, I couldn't contain myself and hastily called my sister, Carole. As the phone rang and rang, my hands would not stop trembling. Please, Carole, answer your damn phone!

"Can this really be happening?" I thought to myself. "Will I really have my grandchild with me every day and night?"

When Carole finally answered, I read her the text, and she simply said, "God does answer our prayers, doesn't He?"

"It took Him way too long, though!" I replied.

"Mattie, you know as well as I do, that He answers in His own time and in His own way. And, you now have your answer, don't you? What are the next steps?"

"First off, I need to go find David and make sure he's okay with this huge responsibility. Then, if he gives his blessing, I'll call Ethan."

"Good luck with everything, Mattie. Call me anytime you need, okay?"

"I will, Carole. And thanks for always being my go-to person. Talk to you soon. Bye."

I thought to myself how odd it was that just a few weeks ago David and I were not good enough to be a part of this child's life. Yet now Megan was asking us to adopt our grandchild. Whatever her reasoning, I sure wasn't going to question this new direction any further.

Wanting to find David to tell him, I ran outside and quickly heard the tractor in the vicinity of the back pasture. Hopping on the golf cart, I hurried to his location and began urgently waving at him until I caught his attention.

Shutting down the tractor, he said, "What is it? Is Poppa okay?"

"Yes, he's fine. But I have other news that you are not going to believe. Megan wants us to adopt our grandchild!"

"What the hell? That's not what she indicated a couple weeks ago. I wonder what changed her mind?"

"I have no idea, David, but would you be okay with this? I really want to say yes, but I'm scared. We're not in our prime anymore, and it is a huge and exhausting responsibility to care for and raise a child. Do you think we can handle this responsibility.?"

David just looked down at me from the tractor and said, "Oh my God, yes!"

The vision of him saying yes is still embedded in my memory.

Now that I had David's blessing, I called Ethan. Of course, he didn't pick up, so I texted him and said, "Answer your phone, dammit. I have some great news."

Ethan picked up immediately when I called a few seconds later. As I told him the news, he broke down crying.

"She never told me," Ethan sniffled. "Why wouldn't she share this decision with me?"

"I have no idea, son. I'm sure her parents may have something to do with it. My question is this: Would you be okay with it? Personally, I believe that this is the best direction for your child and our grandchild."

"It sure is, Mom. I love this idea. This way the baby will be with you and Dad, and Megan and I can visit and be a part of his or her life as well."

"Absolutely, Ethan."

Since I had everyone's blessing regarding the pending adoption, I felt my mind and body lighten. The dark chains of sadness that had bound me for so many months crumbled and broke away.

I glanced at myself in the mirror before texting Megan back, and I saw my eyes start to sparkle once again. They were no longer dull. I felt alive. I had something to live for!

Grabbing my phone, I responded to Megan's text. "Megan, David and I would love to adopt our grandchild. We are ecstatic that you asked us. It is an answer to our prayers." And then I added, "Remember, no matter what, that our entire family will always welcome you in your child's life."

Megan responded with a thumbs-up emoji, and within a week, their family lawyer called me.

When I answered his call, he briefly stated that we would receive the adoption papers within the week, and once we filled them out, we should return them in the prepaid envelope that would be included.

"Certainly. That would be fine," I said. We'll get those completed and send them back ASAP."

Can I say I was giddy with excitement? Umm, yes, I was.

In a few days, the documents arrived.

And my giddiness abruptly subsided.

As I read through the legalese, it became suddenly and horribly apparent to me that it excluded Ethan from any decisions regarding his child.

What the hell?

Simply put, the adoption documents explicitly stated that the adoptee father would be David R. Hill and the adoptee mother would be Mattie T. Hill. It further stated that Ethan C. Hill, my son, would not be allowed any jurisdiction over the adopted child.

Reading this hurt me to the core as a mother, not only because it would be a devastating blow to Ethan but also because I realized that we had failed our son. As I said earlier, Ethan was and always would be a free spirit. Smart, witty, charming, and loving to a fault, he had always wanted to take the easy and fun road, which led him to making some very poor life choices.

Obviously, some of these choices had come back to bite him, big time. I wondered what David and I could have done differently raising Ethan. And then I questioned myself as to whether we truly would be good parents to our grandchild. I quickly pushed that thought out of my mind.

I have never told Ethan any of the wordage in the adoption papers.

Nor did I tell David as I watched him sign the documents.

The signed documents were sent off in the mail the next day.

And then it was done. We would have our grandchild with us in a month.

Several days later, I suggested to David that we hire a lawyer so we would have protection.

"We don't need a lawyer," he replied bluntly.

"Yes, dear, we do. We need someone that is familiar with family law and the adoption process to be our spokesperson. I don't know anything about it. Do you?

"Well, no. Where are we going to find a lawyer?"

"I'll ask around," I answered.

The next day I spent hours on the phone, calling friends and business acquaintances to ask if they could recommend someone. No one that I spoke with had any experience with what we were going through. In desperation, I turned to Google.

My search results listed way too many options. I called the first number and was put on hold. I hung up. I called the next number and was greeted by automation. I hung up. On the third call, a lovely female voice answered the phone.

"Hello, my name is Diana. How may I help you?"

Hallelujah! A real person.

"Diana, my name is Mattie Hill, and I was wondering if you might be able to help me."

"Well, Mattie, tell me what is going on."

And then, just like that, the flood gates opened, and I told my new comrade in arms what was going on. I must have rattled on for over a half hour.

After, I was done, Diana simply said, "Mattie, we can help."

Hallelujah!

After we confirmed an appointment for the following day to speak with the lawyer, I hung up with Diana and went to look for David.

I found him out back under the gazebo having a cocktail.

When he looked at me, he said, "You look mad."

"David, I have hired a lawyer."

"Okay, but why do you look mad?"

"I'm mad because I feel like I'm the only one fighting for our grandchild."

"What in the world are you talking about? I have told you time and again, I'll back you and back Ethan. I signed the adoption papers, didn't I?"

"Yes, you did. But I'm the only one doing anything. I'm the one researching lawyers. I'm the one communicating with Megan, I'm the middleman between Megan and Ethan, and I'm struggling right now. David, I feel like everyone is leaving it up to me to make this situation right."

David took a sip of his cocktail and, as he put the glass down, he looked at me sternly and said, "Mattie, you're the one who always needs to be in control. You have never asked for my help, so I have learned to just leave you alone until you do ask me."

Well, crap. Didn't he bust my bitch rant?

And he was right.

I sat down in the chair next to him under the gazebo, and as the soft-pastel twilight sky painted itself into the rich umbrella of the southern night's celestial heavens, I asked David for his help.

The following day, both David and I spoke with our newly hired lawyer via telephone. After numerous questions from both David and me—mainly David— he reminded us that many young mothers often change their minds about adoption after the birth of their child. "Not to worry," I told him. "Megan is the one who initiated this. She hasn't even given the baby a name yet, for goodness sakes!"

Our lawyer, Joseph Vincent, just reiterated his warning and finished up the conversation by asking us to send a copy of our signed documents to his office, which we did the next day.

With no news from the other party, David and I went shopping.

We shopped for all the baby necessities needed for bringing a newborn home. We purchased the safest car seat and a beautiful stroller. We spent almost an hour testing out the strollers. Were they easy to open and collapse? Were they heavy and cumbersome? Were they easy to clean? After finally deciding on the right one, we paid for all our purchases and headed home. It was a very happy day for David and me.

After all the shopping needs were met, we filled our days with painting the nursery a beautiful sea-foam blue (yes, we finally were told it was a boy), hanging new curtains, and placing family keepsakes for our grandchild to enjoy as he grew. We pulled out our great-grandfather's iron crib from the attic and gave it a thorough sanding. To complete it, we painted it an antique white. It turned out beautifully and looked lovely against the new color on the walls. I purchased a lovely crib set with ocean colors that also complemented the wall color and a mobile of dolphins to hang over the crib. The final touch for the nursery was a mahogany rocker that my mother used to rock all her children, including me. I reupholstered it in a soft green, white, and blue striped fabric that reminded me of the ocean, and when David and I placed the newly revitalized chair in the room, we knew our grandchild's nursery was complete.

It was perfect.

As the news spread that our grandchild would be coming home to us, family members sent special mementos to include in the nursery. They dropped off nursery pictures that had graced their children's nursery walls; family photos, beautifully framed; silver baby spoons and forks; teething rings; and one-of-a-kind nursery books, just to name a few. And, of course, loads and loads of diapers. Friends and neighbors dropped off layette items, bottles, formula, toys, and beautiful stuffed animals to surround our grandchild with love. All this outpouring of care from our family and friends was confirmation that it truly does take a village to raise a child.

My dream was coming true.

David and I were overjoyed with the support and love that surrounded us. It was amazing! So many people had stepped up and supported us as we waited to welcome our grandchild into our family.

I had found myself again. I would turn the radio on in the car and sing to all my favorite songs. I hummed as I greeted Poppa in the morning at the breakfast table. One morning he said to me, "Happy looks good on you, Mattie."

I skipped over to him and gave him a happy kiss on his withered, whiskered cheek, giggling. "Thank you, Poppa. I am happy."

All the previous bad encounters were now a distant memory. David had said many times over the past months, "Everything will work out," and I was finally starting to believe him.

David and I went through the final weeks of Megan's pregnancy in a happy daze, purchasing the last-minute items needed for the nursery. We never felt closer. We were both united in this common cause. We held hands a lot during this time as we sat under the manor's gazebo and talked about our future with our grandson. Our lives had a renewed purpose, and we were thriving on it! He would be with us soon, and life was good.

Chapter 14

It's funny how you begin an ordinary day not expecting the extraordinary to occur. But that morning was just that. It was a typical late-winter morning in the South. A light frost tipped the few green blades of grass on the front lawn still vigilantly clinging to life. The green on the trees existed only on the magnolias, the live oak, and the pine trees. It seemed as if everything in nature was just resting a bit, saving up its energy to emerge into the spring grandeur that the South would unfold in just a few months.

In the kitchen, the coffee was brewing, and the tea-kettle was beginning to boil. David and I were busy with our normal morning chores. I had finished feeding the horses, and David had just come in for a cup of coffee after feeding the dogs. I asked him what his plans were for the day. "Oh, the same old stuff. There's a broken board along the frontage road pasture that needs to be fixed, so I think I'll start with that," he replied. "How about you? Will it be busy at work today?"

Between sips of my hot tea, I answered, "I'm pretty much caught up, which is wonderful. I just love checking things off my to-do list as completed and done!"

David chuckled and said, "You do love having all your ducks in a row. It keeps you organized and prepared."

Smiling, I answered him. "Someone has to stay on top of things around here."

Little did I know that, in a short while, I would truly find out about what having all my ducks in a row meant. I gave David a quick kiss and went outside to the barn to let the horses out to graze for the day. I cleaned up their stalls and got their feed buckets cleaned in preparation for their evening meal and headed back to the house.

Have you ever been so prepared for something that when the actual time comes to respond, you're at a total loss for what to do? Well, that happened just a few minutes later when I was walking back from the stable and heard David hollering for me from the back deck.

Thinking he was hurt, or Poppa was having a medical emergency, I quickly ran up to the deck. "What's wrong? Is everything okay?" I asked.

"It's time," he said.

"Time for what?" I replied, dumbfounded.

He looked at me incredulously and said, "Our grandchild is coming, and soon!"

I had our bags and the baby's bag packed for at least a month—okay, maybe two—yet I ran around the house as if I were that exuberant expectant father. I couldn't find a bloody thing! All my organization, planning, and lists had gone out the window! Ducks in a row: that's a laugh! There was no row of ducks happening at that moment!

"Our grandchild will be home soon," I thought as I frantically tried to find all the carefully packed belongings. David was trying not to be impatient with me. I was looking for this and that, and when I asked him where everything was, he said, "Just where you left them."

"But where the hell is that?" I asked.

David looked at me and said, "Mattie, everything is packed in his nursery closet, just where you placed it two months ago."

Let me tell you, this was a true reversal of roles in our marriage! David telling me where things were; that was a first!

Anyway, I finally got my act together and grabbed the bags, and we hopped in the car for the five-hour drive. I was hoping beyond hope that we would make it there before our grandchild made his official debut. "Do you think we'll get there in time?"

"Of course, we will. Everything will be fine," replied David. As always, he was the positive one.

Thankfully, it was so early in the morning when we left that we were on the interstate before rush hour. That fact kept me somewhat peaceful. Of course, every vehicle that got in front of us or didn't allow us to pass had me in a fit of nervous energy. "Come on, David. Get around him! We won't be there in time" became my manic mantra for the next several hours.

David continued to be patient with me. He was funny like that. The really important events or major life issues regarding our children or any life situation: he handled those easily. Unfortunately, I became this tightly twisted hellion that couldn't remain calm even if I was loaded up with lots of those special gummies that are so popular these days! I believed it was because of his military training, but also it was because David was logical, which was completely opposite of me: a highly sensitive, emotional female. Over the years he had somehow figured out how to keep me in balance. But I must tell you, if he got mad...Katie, bar the door! No one would be safe from an ear chewing. And the ear chewing would be long, and very descriptive!

We continued towards our destination, one peaceful, the other constantly fidgeting and checking her cell phone for any updates and yelling at every car that got in our way.

Halfway through our journey, there were no longer those irritating vehicles in front of us slowing our progress, so I took the opportunity to go over the list in my head to see if I had everything needed to bring our grandchild home. Double-checking our grandson's bag that was securely by my feet, I saw we had lots of diapers, wipes, going-home clothes, bottles, and formula. Then I happened to glance at the back seat. There, securely fastened, was the empty car seat that David and I joyfully purchased several weeks ago. It was just waiting for our little one to fill it. Thinking of our ride home in just seventy-two hours, my heart just danced, imagining our grandchild there, securely nestled, beginning his life with us. We would be bringing our grandbaby home! I must surely have been glowing with anticipation, just like all new mothers, I thought.

Looking over everything in the car that we had prepared just for him, I couldn't contain the happy tears that crept from the corner of my eyes. After all the turmoil of the previous months, my fervent prayers had finally been answered, and our new adventure was soon to become our new normal. As I wiped the moisture from my eyes, my thoughts returned to his nursery that we had so lovingly decorated. It was filled with so much family history that I couldn't wait for the day to tell our grandson the story about the plane from his great-uncle that hung over his crib, or the rocking chair that sat in the corner of his room that belonged to his great-grandmother. And that the crib he would sleep in as an infant originally belonged to his great-great-great-grandfather. When he graduated from the crib, he would sleep in a ship captain's bed made of mahogany and signed by the carpenter. It had belonged to his great-great-great-grandmother and had come all the way from England. All this family history I would tell our grandchild as I lulled him gently to sleep in my mother's rocking chair.

Then I envisioned us, him more grown, walking together along the wooded trails of the family property, surrounded by the quiet solitude of the forest, me telling him the history of the property and the stories of all the relatives that made him so very special. It was a glorious daydream as we traveled the highway to the hospital, ready to meet him for the first time.

We were about forty minutes away, and I was feeling fairly confident that we would make it in time. We had not experienced a flat tire or any engine or traffic issues, and thankfully we hadn't gotten a speeding ticket. We were going to make it! Suddenly my phone chimed with an incoming message from Ethan. "Where are you?"

"We're almost there," I replied. "Is everybody okay? We'll be there within the half hour."

Ethan texted, "You need to get here quickly."

I sent up a quick prayer: "Dear Lord, please get us there in time." Turning to David, I implored him to step on it. "I don't care what you have to do; we have to get to the hospital quickly," I stated firmly. As David increased our vehicle's speed, I truly believed we had guardian angels watching over us that morning. We finished the next thirty miles in record time without any incidents.

Suddenly, I can't keep my thoughts from wandering. It's time to stop writing, so I look over what I jotted down over the last several days, do some editing and then some more editing. I am happy with what I have written and thankfully remember to save my story. I sure don't want to lose what I have penned.

I decide I deserve a glass of wine...maybe two!

After heading to the kitchen, I rinse out my coffee cup, place it in the dishwasher, and grab a wineglass to fill with my well-deserved wine. I pour myself a hefty portion of my favorite Shiraz, grab the bottle, and go out back to sit on the back deck.

Looking over my back yard, I realize I have really let the garden go. Weeds are everywhere. The bird feeder is empty and hanging askew from its shepherd's hook. Sipping my wine, I make a mental note that as soon as I finish my story, my next project will be in my yard.

I've been sitting out back for several hours, enjoying my wine and the night air and the peacefulness that I'm experiencing.

"It's well deserved," I think to myself. "I've earned some solitude. But it's time to put the wine away and get some sleep so you have a clear head to continue writing tomorrow."

Chapter 15

We arrived at the hospital and easily found a parking space since it was just midmorning. David parked the car, and even though time was of the essence, we instinctively reached for each other's hands before leaving the car. Not saying a word, we just held hands tightly. Words were not necessary. There was not a cloud in the sky this special January morning, and the sun was just peeking above the hospital roofline, hinting at the new life of the day and the new life of our grandchild that would be arriving soon. It was a brilliant sunrise. I knew what I was longing for was about to happen, and I hoped David was truly on board with this challenge.

Shifting my position slightly in the front seat, I glanced at him. I looked at his free hand, which was resting on the steering wheel, and I saw how weathered it was. And I saw how his face had become deeply lined and rough from all the outdoor work over the past several years. I watched quietly as a single joyful teardrop welled up and spilled from the corner of his eye. I reached over and gently wiped it away and leaned in for a soft kiss. He turned toward me, and instantly we both broke into grins that spoke of the overabundance of joy that our future now promised.

"This is it," he said. "Are you ready?"

"I've known for months that I'm ready for this," I eagerly replied.

"You sure have, and that's what always amazes me about you: you're always there for our kids, no matter what. You'll move heaven and earth, or whatever is in your power, to be there for our children. And now you are doing it for our grandchild," David replied.

Without hesitation, I answered, "In our own individual ways, we both do that, David." We gathered our grandchild's belongings and headed for the hospital entrance and to our new life with our new child.

The hospital doors swished open with a soft, gentle hiss, and as I walked through the glass doors, I noticed that even at this early hour, there were smudge prints of the hands that had passed before me. I wondered if these souls were entering to welcome a new life into this world or saying goodbye to one that was about to depart. So many doors we walk through, never really knowing what the outcome will be.

Our potential outcome was intoxicating for me. We were about to welcome our new child into this world.

I felt like the queen surveying and nodding to her subjects as I walked into that hospital foyer (unfortunately, there were no subjects in the hospital entrance at the time, but that didn't matter). And I walked that way; tall, secure, and proud. That in and of itself is amazing, since I am a very short, petite woman. But I felt like I was five-foot-ten-inches tall that morning. The smile on my face as I entered must have broken all world records. My child was about to arrive! I was so over-the-moon happy. I had known about this baby for so long; I had waited for this baby for so long. And now he was on the way. David looked at me like I was a lunatic, but I knew he understood. He was just as happy.

Walking toward the elevators to the maternity ward on the third floor, I grabbed David's arm and steered him toward the gift shop.

"What are you doing?" he said.

"We can't go up to Megan empty handed," I answered. "This is one of the biggest days in her life, and we need to let her know that we acknowledge her as part of our family, thank her, and understand and support her." Naturally, he gave me another one of those "Mars will never understand Venus" looks, grumbled, and waited patiently as I selected a beautiful bouquet of flowers and a sweet blue newborn cap with their school insignia embroidered on it.

As I collected the items to bring to the cashier, I wondered about Megan and what she was going through at that moment. I recalled when I was carrying my children that I wanted nothing more than to see their little faces and that nothing on this earth could ever separate them from me. She had carried her child for nine months, so how can she let him go, I wondered. Please God, continue to answer our prayers.

We paid for our items and headed toward the elevator. As I pushed the button for the maternity floor, I felt my heart thumping against my ribs, as if it were about to break through them with excitement and, yes, also fear. It seemed like forever, waiting for this day, and now it was happening so quickly. So many things could go wrong, I thought. But no, we had everything in writing, and all parties had put their signatures on the dotted line. We were good to go. Our grandchild would soon come home with us.

The elevator doors finally opened, and we stepped in. I felt my anxiety escalate as we traveled upward to the maternity floor. Yet at the same time, a soft light also grew inside me, because I knew that this little being was preparing to say hello.

Lord, how I ached to see him. I had purchased so many things for him. David had been irritated with me, but I couldn't stop myself. I was bringing my grandson home, our son home, and I needed to have everything ready.

I had the gifts that I had purchased from the hospital gift store for Megan, as well as another special gift.

David saw me pull a velvet pouch out of my purse and asked me, "What is that, Mattie?"

"It's the string of pearls that my godmother gave me. I thought it would be a nice thing to give to Megan for entrusting her son to us."

"Mattie, it's obvious she does not care about our family keepsakes. Those pearls won't me a thing to her and they should go to Claire."

"David, don't you think she'd like them?"

"No, Mattie. She returned the engagement ring; she sure wouldn't care about a string of pearls. Those pearls belong to Claire and no one else."

As the elevator doors swooshed open, I tucked the velvet pouch back in my purse. David was right. I was silly to think a string of pearls from my family would compensate her for giving her child to us.

We walked onto the maternity floor, and a nurse stopped us to ask whom we were visiting. We told the nurse, and we were guided down the hall to Megan's room. Opening the door, I saw Ethan by Megan's side, and Megan's parents were sitting by the window. I hugged my son, hugged Megan, and walked over to acknowledge Megan's parents. I gave her mother a gentle hug, which she didn't reciprocate, and then went to hug her father. He quickly held out his hand, blocking my attempt to hug him. Looking him straight in the eyes, I ignored his hand and hugged him anyway. That aura of anger that they showed us months ago still emanated from both parents, and it landed squarely on me, my son, and my husband. There was no way that I could help them with their anger. It was their choice to react this way, not mine. I had accepted their behavior to this point and acknowledged that it was their right to feel the way they did. But it didn't mean I had to behave as they did. Yet it hurt me to my very core. As David always said, everyone likes you, Mattie. But Megan's parents sure didn't. David just acknowledged them with a nod.

We settled into our opposing corners of Megan's labor and delivery room. Awkwardly, I attempted to start some sort of conversation. To say it was uncomfortable was an understatement. Quickly, David and I realized that it was silly to even try to be sociable, so we stopped trying.

Ethan was holding Megan's hand, and both were quietly talking to one another. Megan then asked me to take a picture of her and Ethan together, so I acquiesced. Furious, Megan's mother got up, walked across the room and grabbed my arm stating that I was not allowed to post anything on social media. I replied crisply, "This is your daughter's phone, and she asked me to take a picture. It's up to her what she posts. Could you please just put your personal feelings aside and think of your daughter? And kindly remove your hand from my arm." Ethan and David were dumbfounded, and Megan looked aghast, watching as I continued to stand up for myself against her mother. Little did I know that there would be many more emotional confrontations waged against each other in the not-so-distant future.

That catfight was over, and just in time. The maternity nurse shooed David, me, and Megan's father out of the room to check on Megan's progress. In just a few moments, the nurse exited the room and told us that we could not go back in because our grandson would be arriving very soon. Megan wanted only her mother and Ethan in the room, so we settled ourselves in the maternity waiting area, once again commencing on another series of clumsy exchanges of conversation. Quickly we resorted to silence and waited. It was the most comfortable choice, considering the situation.

We were the only people waiting for a new arrival that morning, so thankfully the strained stillness didn't seem so overbearing. We didn't suffer too long in the silence. Ethan walked down the hall about twenty minutes later with this goofy grin on his face punctuated by glistening tears. "He's here! And everyone is okay!"

David and I jumped up, overjoyed, and hugged our son, so happy that it was an uncomplicated birth, considering the dispirited pregnancy. Feeling Megan's father's isolation as he stood there alone, I walked to him, reached up, and hugged him, saying, "Your little girl is okay." He seemed grateful and actually welcomed my embrace! "Well, that's a sign in the right direction," I thought.

Thirty minutes later, we were allowed back in Megan's room. It seemed that with our grandson's arrival, the strained atmosphere that was present forty minutes before had dissipated, and we were all enthralled by this new little being. I got my first glance of him in his mom's arms. He was very small but perfect. Megan seemed detached, but I attributed that to being tired after giving birth. Perhaps it was a good thing, since I would be taking him home with me in seventy-two hours. I wasn't going to fret about that right now.

All the grandparents got a chance to hold him, and as Ethan handed him to me, I cradled him close to my heart. "You are mine, little one. No matter where you are or who you are with, you are my soul. And now that you are here, I will never let you go. You are a part of me," I whispered quietly in his ear. I knew this in my heart and in the deepest depths of my being, that this baby and his spirit were part of me. I couldn't explain it to anyone as I held him; I just knew it. I felt it just as if I had given birth to him. Our connection was strong, and I thanked God for it, since he was going to be my son.

About an hour later, they moved Megan to her recovery room. In a few moments we were ushered into her room, just David, Ethan and me. We spent a few wonderful hours together. Megan's parents had left to give us family time, which was an assumption on my part, but I was grateful. And miraculously, Megan seemed to be happy to have just us with her.

Late in the afternoon, David and I reluctantly left the hospital for the hotel. Truthfully, we were exhausted. Ethan opted to stay with Megan and his son at the hospital.

After entering our hotel room, my husband and I collapsed on the bed and fell immediately to sleep. Just before I crashed, I remember how extremely happy I felt that we seemed to be getting along well with Megan's parents and everyone was handling your arrival with maturity. "Perhaps everything will work out," I murmured to David. "That certainly would be a change and a blessing." David didn't reply as he softly snored. And then I slept, a deep and well-deserved sleep.

I woke up early the next morning, so excited to greet the day. David was taking way too long to wake up, so I left the room and went to the lobby for a cup of tea and to check in with Claire at home. I knew she'd be up, since she had flown home yesterday afternoon to stay with Poppa and take care of the animals. Dialing the number and waiting for her to answer, I thought of the car seat securely buckled in our vehicle and what the next forty-eight hours would bring. Oh boy—literally, oh boy—he'll be coming home! Claire picked up and asked how everything was.

"Fine," I replied. "He is perfect. A little small, but all his tests are good."

"When will you be bringing him home?" Claire asked.

"In thirty-six hours," I replied. "Isn't it so exciting?"

We chatted about inane things, such as the mail and what the dogs had chewed up that day. With the call ended and my tea finished, I headed back up to our room. David was up, dressed, and ready for breakfast.

"Breakfast? We don't need to eat; we need to go see our grandchild!" I exclaimed.

"Please slow down. We need to live our lives normally, alright?" David stated. "At least let me get a cup of coffee before we head back to the hospital."

I agreed, but inside, my mind and my body were nothing close to normal, as once again I squirmed in my chair while David finished that damn cup of coffee!

My grandchild was coming home soon! No, that wasn't right. My *baby* was coming home soon!

David and I buckled into the car for the short trip to the hospital. I couldn't wait to gather him in my arms again. He was such a tiny bundle, and I just loved looking at his sweet face.

We arrived at the hospital, and once again I ran into the gift shop.

"What in the world are you doing now?" David demanded.

"I saw a beautiful blue wreath that I want to get to hang on Megan's door. All the other maternity doors have a wreath, and I don't want her to feel isolated." I made my purchase, and we took the elevator up to Megan's room. Ethan was there, holding his son while sitting on the bed next to Megan.

Ethan and I hugged, and I showed Megan the wreath. She loved it and said to hang it on her door. I was so happy she liked it; it was an affirmation that she approved of the steps I was taking to make her feel comfortable and cared for.

I hung the wreath on her door, and it looked wonderful. Now her door was adorned, just like all the other new mothers'. Yet I couldn't dwell on the maternity doors any longer; I just had to hold my grandson, so I rushed back into the room. Ethan was still holding him, and as soon as I walked over, he handed the baby over to me, and I felt his warm little body snuggle up to my chest. I was in absolute heaven. His little lips would purse up, and he would reach for me instinctively with his hands. I gladly grasped his little ones in mine. He was so content with me, and I was so content to nurture him and be there for him. I felt our bond grow stronger, just as I am sure he did.

As the day drew on, I had an opportunity to visit with Megan one on one. Ethan and Megan still hadn't chosen a name. Ethan left to get something to eat, and as I held the baby, Megan and I sat together, side by side, on the sofa in the hospital room.

"Megan, what are you going to name the baby?"

"Ethan and I agreed on Jeremy."

I thought the name was perfect. In the Old Testament, it is a name often mentioned, and in Hebrew it means "God will uplift."

"Perfect," I said, "What about his middle name?" She hung her head and said she didn't care. I looked at her a bit dumbfounded by this reply and inquired about her father's middle name. She told me it was Crawford. "That's a beautiful name," I stated.

"How about Jeremy Crawford Hill; it's a wonderful and strong name, full of biblical and family history."

Megan liked that idea.

At last, my grandson had a name. My child had a name.

We spent the rest of the morning taking photos of everyone and opening the gifts we had brought for Megan. Megan's mom arrived later in the day and handed me a huge gift bag. Surprisingly, her face seemed softer as I thanked her and opened the gift bag. In it was a collection of day sleepers, bottles, diapers, and other necessities, as well as Jeremy's first Bible. As I pulled each precious item out, I thought to myself how much things had changed over the past few hours. With this little boy's arrival, a welcomed harmony between our two opposing families seemed to ensue. What a wonderful outcome. God did listen!

We left the hospital that day, one step closer to bringing our boy home. After settling into the hotel room after dinner, both David and I fell once again into an exhausted sleep.

The next morning the early dawn light glinted through the drawn hotel room drapes, teasing my eyes to open. As I woke up, I was filled with such happiness just knowing that I would bring my grandson home on that day. In all honesty, I really didn't sleep much during the night. I lay awake, wondering what the future would hold for Jeremy Crawford Hill and whether David and I really could handle caring for an infant and raising a child at our age. It was a bit overwhelming, but oh so worth it! Today was the day I would buckle him into the car seat and take him home to his special nursery. Wow! There are no words in the dictionary to explain how I felt. It felt like home. It felt right. I felt content.

Years ago, I had the same feeling when I brought my children home from the hospital. The excitement, the contentment, the worry at being a parent, all rolled into one emotion. The complete emotion is one of undying love for another human being. It is the commitment of nurturing and caring for someone that looks to you for everything. It is the love of a parent for their child.

In the wee hours of that morning, it seemed to me as if God was saying to David and me, "I will trust you with this gift because you are wiser, you have traveled this road, and you both give unconditional love to your children."

Ethan had spent the night with Megan again, so David and I just grabbed a quick cup of coffee and a Danish to eat before we rushed happily off to the hospital. The beautiful dawn light that I had witnessed just a few hours ago had now turned into a cold, gray day with heavy ominous clouds, and I sent up a quick prayer that this was not an omen of things to come. Thinking back, I should have prayed a lot harder, because our day was about to turn to shit.

We arrived around 9:00 a.m. that morning. Ethan was already there, but he was sitting in the waiting room with his head hanging low. "What's going on?" I asked. He looked at me in bewilderment and said that he didn't have a clue. "Is everyone okay?" All he could tell me was that Megan wanted some time on her own. "Where's Jeremy?" I asked.

"He's in the room with Megan," Ethan replied.

I was still in such a state of euphoria, just knowing that he was coming home with me today: my little one, the boy that I had loved from the moment I heard about him; my heartbeat, my future. But in that euphoric state,

I was blind to the red flags flapping frantically in front of my face. None of it registered as I walked to the nurse's station to inquire about the paperwork that would release Jeremy to us. They informed me that I needed to get the paperwork from Megan, so I went back to the waiting room where David and Ethan were. Neither had any more information. Unaware of what was going on, I just couldn't let it go, so I went to Megan's room.

I gently knocked on the closed door that displayed the sweet blue baby wreath that I had bought the day before. Megan's mother opened the door, and I asked if I could come in and visit. To my absolute horror, she said, "No."

I simply asked, "Why?"

"My daughter doesn't want you here." And she harshly slammed the door in my face.

I stood there, dumbfounded, for several minutes, just staring at that closed door with the blue wreath. My mind went numb. My heart went numb. What in the world were these people doing? Why were they treating us like this? What had we done wrong? All these thoughts ran through my head in a dialogue of confused, nonlogical thoughts. My mind was filled with such an emotional turmoil that I just wanted to collapse on the floor and scream in outrage at the cruelty of what had just transpired. They had sucker punched us once again. I stood broken, looking blankly at that closed door for what seemed like an eternity.

Finally, I gathered my wits, and in a fury, I went back to the waiting room where Ethan and David still sat and told them what had happened. As usual, when I'm totally losing control, David tried to calm me. This time, his platitudes did not work. I began to pace and to rant. And while I ranted, Ethan withdrew further into himself. Looking back on it, I should have gone to Ethan and consoled him, but I was so angry at being treated with such disrespect that I couldn't even think about someone else's feelings, even my son's. I wanted to find a protective, warm chamber and surrender to its warmth. I wanted my mom. I wanted to feel her protective arms envelop me and tell me in her soft, lyrical British accent that everything would be fine. But my mother had passed long ago, and there was no lyrical British accent to soothe me, nor was there anyone else that could squash my rising panic.

As bad as this latest situation was, it was about to get even worse.

I continued to wear a path in the carpet from my pacing. I was truly trying to get a grip on what had just transpired and how to handle it. Okay, I was not doing a good job of it. I was raging on the inside and shaking on the outside. I had never been treated like this in all my life. I glanced over at Ethan and David, both still sitting miserably in the waiting room chairs. Our once bright and brilliant day of bringing you home had now turned to darkness. Oh, those ominous clouds; how I should have heeded their visual warning!

Suddenly, the elevator doors opened, and two security guards exited onto the floor. None of us even noticed them. Oddly, the guards approached David and Ethan. I was still walking frantically back and forth, so I did not see them or hear the conversation they had with my husband and son.

David walked over to me and grabbed my arm. I glared at him as he told me that we had to leave the hospital.

"What are you talking about? Why do we have to leave?" I shouted at David. "We are just here in the waiting room. We are not doing anything wrong!" David calmly told me we needed to leave.

I needed to know why. I could not remain silent. David and Ethan by then had completely removed themselves from me because they knew that I had just lost my last bit of control. How can I simply walk away, away from a child that is supposed to be mine, without some sort of explanation?

Completely exploding with anger, I strode over to the two soft, overweight hospital guards until I was inches from their faces and demanded a reason. They simply replied like robots: "Ma'am, you must leave the premises, or we will physically remove you and your family."

"You have to tell me why," I screamed at them. When one of the guards put his hand on me to physically guide me towards the elevator, David pulled me away. I didn't want to be pulled away, because I really wanted to slug somebody. Truthfully, I wanted to sucker punch those guards, or anybody that was in my nearby vicinity, just like we had been sucker punched. I was visibly shaking with anger, and my blood was boiling with hate.

I wanted to collapse onto the dirty waiting room carpet and scream obscenities that no good Catholic girl would say. I wanted everyone to hear my pain, especially the people that were sitting in *my* baby's hospital room.

However, I did not collapse; nor did I scream obscenities. I remained standing, with David's hand on my shoulder. As I pushed my shoulders back, standing as tall as my broken spirit would allow, I looked directly in both hospital guards' eyes with rage and told them both, "Kiss my ass! We're leaving, and don't you friggin' touch me again!"

David and Ethan guided me to the elevator that I had so happily traveled in just an hour ago. I saw nothing. My eyes were blurred with rage. I don't even remember leaving the hospital.

I didn't reach for my son; I didn't even reach for my husband. I just shut myself down in a protective cocoon, hoping that, somehow, I would no longer feel the pain or the anger. But that pain and anger never left. We had been rejected. Once more, and quite literally, they slammed the door in our face and nonverbally said we were not good enough.

What just happened to me felt like the unexpected death of a loved one that you never saw coming. You keep breathing; you keep walking. Your eyes blink, and you communicate, but you aren't living. You become an actor in the play of life, never showing anybody the full extent of your loss and what it has done to you and your family.

I was done. I was cold and bitter. I had nothing. They killed my joy, my spirit, and my soul. I had no more strength to fight them. The fire that was Mattie had been extinguished. I was nothing. Hadn't they just told me that?

I now know why I had those several glasses of wine last night. I don't want to remember this part of the story. It hurts so badly to recall that day and to put the memories down on paper. Writing this part of my story is not therapeutic. It feels as if someone has just ripped the stitches out of my slowly healing heart and left it openly bleeding and struggling to beat another heartbeat.

That day was supposed to be a beautiful homecoming, but instead it became one of the worst days of my life. Or so I thought—in a few short years, they would deliver an even more malignant decision for us to deal with.

No wine tonight, because writing these memories down has worn me out.

I'll just go outside and sit on the deck and hope that tomorrow I'll be able to deal with the rest of my story in a better fashion.

Chapter 16

We left the hospital in complete silence and despondency. We got back in the van, and the little car seat sat empty, just like our hearts. The dark-gray clouds scattered across the horizon earlier in the day were now heavy, pouring vicious torrents of rain upon us as we drove, bereaved, back to the hotel room. David and I decided not to stay another night in this little town that had become a place of pure hell for our family. We packed up our belongings, along with our grandson's items, checked out of the hotel and started our five-hour journey back to the manor.

Ethan and I exchanged a few words and a hug prior to him getting into his car and proceeding to burn rubber out of the hospital parking lot. I sure hope his guardian angels were there for him in that moment, because his mother was not.

The trip remained silent, except for the rain beating down on the van. It mimicked the torrent of tears that never stopped falling from my eyes the entire journey home. We were all emotionally exhausted and beaten down, but David got us home safely, thank goodness. I had still not spoken a word to him.

I grabbed a big bottle of merlot and a big glass from the bar and immediately went to Jeremy's room. Walking across the nursery threshold, I slammed the door shut and sat in my mother's rocking chair. I uncorked the wine and poured a deep, long glass, hoping to drown my sorrows and anger.

This lovingly created nursery that once held such hope and happiness for me and my family was now a symbol of rejection.

I knew David and Ethan needed me, but I had nothing left to give. I had just been told that our family wasn't worthy again, so wasn't it understandable to feel meaningless and empty? I wanted to be alone and wallow in my complete and utter desolation.

I know I should have considered my husband's and son's feelings. But they were not the ones that had been in constant communication with Megan. They hadn't sent her supportive texts every week. They were not the ones that she had reached out to regarding adoption. I was the one that she had connected with. She had trusted me, and I had trusted her. And now that trust was broken.

The next morning, I opened my eyes to experience a blurred room and a raging wine headache. I had fallen asleep in the nursery rocking chair. I didn't want to greet the day or anyone in it, so I just sat in my mother's chair, gently rocking back and forth, gazing about Jeremy's nursery while the morning sun shone through the windows, wondering what I could have done differently. And wondering what would happen next.

"This morning should have been so different," I thought to myself. Right at this moment, Jeremy should have been cradled in my arms while I fed him a bottle. But that hadn't happened. I sat there with empty arms, trying to figure out how I was supposed to accept this unwanted new normal. And how in the world was my family supposed to get over this unbearable loss? I looked at the adoption papers that I had thrown on the floor the night before and just couldn't understand how this could have happened to us.

I heard David moving about, and I hoped he had fed the animals, because I still didn't want to acknowledge anyone, let alone move out of the nursery and feed animals. Suddenly my cell phone, lying on the floor next to the wrinkled adoption papers, chirped. I reached down for the phone and fumbling to put on my glasses. I read the text that I had just received.

To my astonishment, it was from Megan. You will not believe what her text said! "Where are you?"

Where are we?" I thought to myself. "You fucking kicked us out of the hospital. Where the hell do you think we are?"

Taking a few moments to calm myself down, I texted back. "We are back on the farm. We were asked to leave the hospital per your request, so we went home."

Megan immediately replied, "You're supposed to take him home today. You need to come to my apartment to pick him up."

What the hell is going on with this family? I just couldn't believe that they continued to pull us one way and another. They were like puppet masters constantly pulling our strings as to which way we should move—stay, leave, smile, cry; they had complete control. Taking a few moments to compose myself, I grabbed my phone and got my wine-weary, hungover body out of the rocking chair to go find David.

Finding him in the kitchen with Poppa, I showed him the text. He immediately said, "Let's go." Honestly, part of me didn't want to continue being an unwilling partner in their games anymore. Yet this was my grandchild. I had to do everything I could to be with him.

"David, I am completely exhausted with their game-playing and how they manipulate us at will. I'm really not sure what we should do."

"Mattie, do you still think there is a chance that the adoption will go through?"

"Maybe, but a very slight one," I replied.

"Well, then. Let's hold on to that slight chance and get back there so we can bring our grandbaby home. And don't forget the adoption papers."

I grabbed a quick shower, trying desperately to rinse away the residue of my overindulgent behavior the night before. Once showered and dressed, I grabbed Jeremy's take-home satchel once again, and we set out for another five-hour trip.

About thirty minutes into the drive, I glanced down at our grandson's bag and said to David, "You know, last night I threw Jeremy's bag on the floor in disgust."

"I know you did. I saw you do it before you got your bottle of wine and disappeared."

"I was a mess last night, David. All I could think about was what we would do with everything we bought for him. Should we donate everything, or try to return it? And now, this morning, we are once again heading back, hopefully to bring our grandson home. I sure hope we aren't presented with any more bombshells."

"I hear you. I'm getting close to losing my temper with them."

"In my opinion, it would be well deserved. But please don't, David."

We settled into an anxious silence as the miles drifted by.

About two hours into our drive, Megan texted that she and Jeremy had been released from the hospital and that we should meet her at her apartment. Plugging the address into our GPS, we continued our journey. Our car ride remained quiet. There was so much to say, but David and I were both too damn exhausted by everything that had happened to verbally converse about this new request from our puppet masters. It was completely beyond our understanding. Her family had torn our lives apart on so many occasions over the last several months that I'm sure David and I were thinking along the same lines.

Could we trust them again? What game were they cooking up now? These thoughts and so many kept my mind in a terminal state of chaos during our trip. But deep in the recesses of my heart, I still held on to a glimmer of hope that we would bring Jeremy home.

During the car ride, I called to make another reservation at the same hotel we had checked out of the day before. I called Ethan to tell him about our new directive.

"You have got to be kidding me!" he exclaimed. "We were kicked out of the damn hospital just yesterday!"

"Exactly."

"Yeah, but I haven't had a chance to tell you this bit of news. Megan texted me late last night to let me know it wasn't her idea to kick us out."

"Really. I suppose you're going to tell me it was her mother's?"

"She never indicated that. She just said it wasn't her."

"Did she apologize?" I asked.

"No."

"That doesn't surprise me. Dad and I are already on the road heading back. We're about two and a half hours away and will be checking in at the same hotel as yesterday. Can you meet us there?" I asked.

"Of course, Mom. I want my son with you and Dad."

Two hours later, David and I arrived at the apartment at the time they had designated and gingerly knocked on the door. Megan's mother let us in, and once again her face was set in that rigid and angry mask that I was becoming all too familiar with. I didn't even attempt to hug her; I just said, "Hello," and asked to see Megan.

Megan walked out of her bedroom with Jeremy in her arms. Her demeanor was broken. We had traveled this road together, and we were physically weary and emotionally exhausted from this roller-coaster ride. She walked up to me and placed you in my arms. Tears began to stream down her face. Even with everything that happened yesterday, I couldn't help myself. I gathered her in my arms, with Jeremy between us, and whispered to her that she would always be welcome in his life. As her mother and father stood discreetly in the other room, she let go of him. Megan continued to sob and ran into her bedroom. Her mother walked in from the kitchen and handed me Jeremy's diaper bag, announcing that we had to meet them back at the hospital tomorrow morning at 10:00 a.m. for a well-baby checkup. We thanked them and left the apartment. I could still hear Megan sobbing from her bedroom as the front door slammed behind us.

Walking to the car with you in my arms, I felt no joy. I felt the wounds of a young mother and the wounds of a grandmother that we both had accumulated over the last several months during this journey. I couldn't imagine the pain that Megan was experiencing behind her closed bedroom door. Well, in retrospect, I know that my family and I felt that very same despondency not twenty-four hours earlier. I too had sat behind a closed door the night before, not wanting to communicate or see anyone. I passionately prayed to God that this torment would end for all of us, and soon. But life can be brutal. You never know how many detours, roadblocks, speed bumps, or U-turns you'll have to travel before you find your true direction.

We buckled Jeremy into his car seat, which had been frigid and empty just the day before and headed once again to the hotel. Ethan was scheduled to meet us there within the hour.

During the short drive to our hotel, I said to David, "Do you think Megan is okay?"

"Hell, Mattie, I don't have a clue. That poor girl still doesn't know what she wants to do. Please don't get your hopes up about bringing Jeremy home though. I hate to say it but I'm not feeling positive vibes from our most recent encounter with them."

"Oh God David, what do you mean? Do you think she wants to keep Jeremy? Why would she have us come back up here if she does?" I asked. "I can't handle much more of this craziness!"

"I don't know Mattie," David answered curtly. "I don't know anything right now. Just calm down, okay."

Well, I sure wasn't going to calm down anytime soon, that's for sure.

We settled into our hotel room, and within thirty minutes Ethan arrived. We spent the evening taking turns holding Jeremy and relishing the beauty of him. Ethan said he would take the first shift with Jeremy, so David and I gave Ethan a crash course on the ins and outs of diaper changing and bottle-feeding so we could get some sleep. Around 2:00 a.m., I woke up and found Ethan struggling to settle Jeremy so, tapping my son on his shoulder, I said, "Get some sleep, son. I'll take over now." David was sound asleep, so I placed our grandson between David and me on the bed.

I know, no lecture is necessary: you should never place a baby between two adults. But I did. I gave him a bottle, and after a few moments, he fell peacefully asleep, curled snuggly against my side. I stayed awake the rest of the morning, making sure that neither David nor I rolled on him. I grabbed my cell and took a picture of Jeremy right there, nestled securely next to my heart. I wondered whether, with all the turmoil that Megan's family had assaulted us with, this would be the last time I had you by my side or the first time of many.

We would soon find out.

That next morning, we packed up everything yet again, checked out of the hotel, and set out for Jeremy's well-baby appointment at the hospital. When we arrived, Ethan sat down next to Megan, which was a big surprise to me considering all the animosity that we had all witnessed the other day. Megan seemed restless, so I asked her if she wanted to hold Jeremy, and she immediately took my grandson from my arms. As he left my embrace, my arms suddenly felt so empty, as if a part of my body had been abruptly severed and now was not whole. It took my breath away at how connected I was to him already.

The nurse called Ethan and Megan in for their scheduled appointment, and as the young family went into the room, I finally glanced over at Megan's mother, who had been oddly quiet the whole time. I was suddenly aware that she was not making eye contact with me at all, and my entire being went on high alert. Walking over to her, I took the chair right across from her, so she had to look at me.

"Is there something that I need to know?" I asked. She replied that Megan would talk to me after the appointment.

Well, I had had enough of this calculating maneuvering and their family's way of pulling our strings, so I curtly replied, "No, you owe me an answer, and now. What is going on?"

Not looking at me, she stated softly, "Megan wants to keep the baby." When those words were uttered, my mind did not comprehend the statement fully, but my heart did. Instantly, everything that I'd prepared for, and hoped for, died once again, along with the light that had glimmered just shortly the day before. David, within earshot of the conversation, immediately got up from his chair and left the room. I was grateful for this because obviously he had reached his breaking point. Left alone, I looked out the waiting room window for a few moments, wiping frantically at the river of tears that once again cascaded down my face as I mourned the loss of my child. I had found him, and once again, I had lost him.

As I continued to grieve, staring out the foggy hospital window in complete misery, Megan's mother came over and put her arm around me in a small attempt to console me, but it was way too little and much too late. I shrugged away from her uncomfortable and uninvited embrace and marched right up to the checkup room door where my grandson was and knocked on the door. Not waiting for an answer, I walked straight in while the nurse briskly informed me, "You are not allowed in here."

I fixed her with a determined gaze and said, "Don't worry. I'll just be a minute."

The nurse replied, "No, you have to leave."

"As I said, I'll be just a minute. Telling me to leave is just prolonging my time here. So please let me say what I need to say."

Megan's expression was one of acute apprehension, while Ethan's look was one of complete bewilderment. He had no idea what I had just found out. I knelt in front of Megan, grabbed her hand, and said, "You'll be a great mom, and someday, I hope I can forgive what has happened to my family."

Without glancing at anyone, I stood up, held my head as high as my five-foot frame would allow, and walked out of the room and out of that hospital. As I approached our car, I could see that David was ranting at someone on his cell. I opened the passenger-side door, got in, slammed the door, and proceeded to sob and cuss like a seasoned sailor, all in one fell swoop. Unfortunately, David was still on the phone when I let out my tirade. He was telling his sister, Katie, about the latest turn of events, so she heard me in all my glory!

"Do you want to talk to Katie?" David asked.

I looked at him as if he had two heads. "No, I do not want to talk to anyone."

Ethan came out about a half hour later with Jeremy in his arms. "Lord, what now," I thought. As he put the baby in the car seat, he told us that Megan thought we would like to drive him back to the apartment. Gee, thanks, another ten minutes with the baby that was supposed to be my child. So considerate of them! Let's prolong this agony a wee bit longer.

We buckled Jeremy up and headed back to Megan's apartment. They were there waiting for us. I gathered Jeremy's little suitcase with all the belongings that I had so lovingly purchased months ago and handed the satchel to Megan's mother. I opened the van door, unbuckled Jeremy, and gently kissed him, whispering how much I loved him and how he would always be a part of me. Crying again with no restraint, I turned to Megan and her family and told them exactly what I had whispered to you. "He is a part of me, and I love him with all my heart. Oh, and by the way, you need to get a car seat."

They took Jeremy, and we left for home, once again without our grandson. I wondered if my family and I would ever recover from this ordeal. But I knew we would not. This had changed us all, permanently. We would not be adopting our grandson; nor would we be his guardians. At the time, I had no idea what role we would play in his life.

Chapter 17

Somehow, as the weeks progressed, everyone managed to return to their normal routines of life on the farm. David went through his everyday chores on the property: bush hogging, edging, mowing the riding ring, and mending fences. Secretly, I applauded his fortitude to keep going through the ordinary motions of life, considering our life had been completely turned upside down and inside out.

For me, I would get up and make food for others to eat. I fed the animals, made grocery lists, made appointments for Poppa, and went about the daily chores to keep the house running. I made sure everyone's life was on par. My life, however, was not on par.

Jeremy's stroller, car seat, bottles, clothes and toys had been donated to the local women's pregnancy shelter. David had disassembled the crib and put it back in the attic. My mother's rocking chair was back upstairs. Every item had been either given away or, if it was a family heirloom, the item was sent back with a note of thanks. The nursery was now an empty shell. Just like me.

I thought of him every day. He was the first thought in the morning and the last one in the evening as I lay down to rest. More times than not, he was there in the wee hours of the morning, when my mind was so unsettled that I couldn't sleep.

My invisible wounds refused to heal. Subconsciously, I don't think I wanted them to. I was afraid that if they healed, I would lose Jeremy forever. They were my only reminder of my grandson. Over time, the raw edges mended, but the core of that wound never completely recovered.

We received many phone messages and cards from family and friends, extending their condolences and hopes for peace and understanding. I did appreciate their thoughtfulness, but the words did nothing to ease the constant, aching pain. Many of them stated that it was "God's will" or that "He has a plan." I did not buy into that rhetoric anymore. I did not reply to any of the messages, and the cards were thrown in the trash.

I no longer prayed.

Ethan, too, had lost his focus. He informed us he was quitting school and had decided to join the Marine Corps. He would be leaving in five months for boot camp. Another life altered due to choices made by others.

The weeks progressed into months, and I continued to exist. But there was such a deep vacuum in my soul that I saw none of the beauty of the life around me. I don't know how to explain this darkness. All I knew was that it encompassed me. There was no light in my life, and I was unable to see beyond the blackness. It oozed out of my pores like a black sludge, and I lived that way, continuously, day and night. Heavy with its weight and despair.

Sleep eluded me on a nightly basis. I attempted every known fix: yoga, alcohol, pharmaceuticals, exercise—anything to take me from where I existed now to a place that I could hopefully be peaceful once again. Unfortunately, none of those remedies proved successful.

I did continue to work and take care of the horses, but I had begun to gain weight—and yes, it was mainly due to my daily alcohol consumption. I decided I would join a gym and start swimming. I remember that when I first started swimming, I begged myself to make it six lengths in the pool. Over the next several months, the six lengths graduated to eighteen and then thirty-two. As I swam, I would have conversations with my mom in my head. Most of the time I would tell her about all my concerns, and how I wished she was still here to give me advice. Mainly, I asked her to give me strength. I ached to see her face as I came up for each breath of air. I never saw her, but I always talked to her as I swam. I swam every day. In four months, my pants size was no longer a ten: it was a four. My family and friends began to comment about my weight loss. It didn't matter to me. Plus, it was the one thing I could control at the time. And personally, I didn't give a damn if I wasted away to nothing. Because that's what I felt like—nothing.

Chapter 18

Time passed, and winter gave way to early spring. The farm was once again eagerly announcing the upcoming season. The horse pastures were coming in, green and rich. The azaleas were blooming, and the hummingbirds were back. Their return reminded me of the joy that Mamaw had watching them from the kitchen window, and it did make me smile at the memory.

Several weeks later, I received a text from Megan with a picture of Jeremy and an update from his most recent well-baby checkup. Looking at the text in astonishment, I rushed to find David and gave him my phone to read the text. "Why is she reaching out to me?" I asked David. "How many times do we have to go through this?"

And in his typical fashion, he replied, "Mattie, just text her, and be honest. Don't be emotional. Ask her what she wants from us this time. Don't point fingers at anyone; just thank her for the information and see where it goes from there."

I listened to his advice and sent a thankful, and logical, reply to Megan. Within half an hour she asked if we would like to come visit!

What the hell? They're doing it again, that push-me-pull-me routine that sucks us into their lives. And then, on a whim, they'll decide to abruptly push us back out! I truly couldn't take it anymore, so once again I resorted to my family.

I called Carole and told her the latest.

Carole was ecstatic and said, "What are you waiting for? You want to be in his life, so if you must play on their terms to accomplish that, play their game." "But I just don't know how much more I can take of their acceptance and then their rejection," I replied. Carole, always able to push away all the extraneous things, got to the point. "Do you want to see your grandson?"

Without hesitation I answered, "Of course I do."

Carole replied, "Well, then, there is your decision."

After speaking with my sister, my decision was now crystal clear. I would not worry about anything other than being in my grandson's life. I would play their puppet master games, because being in Jeremy's life was more important to me than anything else. That decided, I texted Megan back and said, "Yes, we would love to visit with Jeremy!"

Via text messages, Megan and I arranged for a visit the following weekend. I told David about the visit, but he said, "Mattie, I'll be there for you, for our son, and for our grandchild, as long as they don't piss me or you off again. I'm just not ready to see any of that family right now." It broke my heart that David had pulled away, but I understood completely. Wasn't I just thinking the same thing twenty-four hours ago?

Once again, I felt contentment returning. I would be back in my grandson's life. I hummed as I worked on clients' projects, smiled as I fed the horses and chatted with Poppa, all because of the anticipation of seeing my grandchild in a few days. Happily, I packed my bag for the trip. Claire was home, so she was coming with me for the weekend.

Megan had left the apartment she had been living in and moved back to her parents' home, so I booked a room at a nearby hotel only five minutes away from her parents' house.

As we left the farm, I kissed David goodbye. He looked deeply into my eyes, telling me without a word that he was with me, and I knew, no matter what, he had my back. As Claire and I drove closer and closer to our destination, my heart began to thump erratically in my chest. Was it the joy of seeing my grandson again, or the worry of what new ultimatum would be laid upon us when we got there? "What's going to happen now?" I wondered.

Claire and I checked into the hotel, showered and got dressed, and left for Megan's house. We arrived at the designated time, and Megan's mother ushered us downstairs, where Megan was living. It was a beautifully appointed basement apartment, complete with kitchen, bathroom, bedroom, and family room. Jeremy was sound asleep in his bassinet. As I gazed at him, Megan's mother commented on all the weight that I had lost, and in my head, I thought, "Well, woman, you and your family's behavior did this to me."

Megan stood in the background as her mother took over. Imagine that! She showed us where the bottles, formula, diapers, and wipes were, and then, to our astonishment, they both headed upstairs, telling us to spend all the time that we wanted with Jeremy. As they disappeared upstairs, Claire and I looked at each other in utter bewilderment at this turnabout. But that only lasted a brief second, as we both grinned wildly and headed over to his bassinet. I gently gathered his little sleeping body into my arms and cradled him against my heart. I felt his heart beating next to mine. I was the happiest I had been in months. I relished feeling the warmth of Jeremy and his gentle breathing as it synchronized with mine.

We spent a wonderful weekend visiting with Jeremy and really enjoyed the company of Megan and her family. Ethan came over that Saturday to spend time with his son and Megan, which completely surprised me. Claire and I happily offered to babysit as they went off for a quiet lunch together. "This is progress," I thought happily. Perhaps this was a sign that our two families could work this situation out amicably.

As the next several months passed, Megan's family and ours had come to a peaceful routine. We were "allowed" to spend one weekend with Jeremy every month. I was thrilled at this solution and happily planned for it every month. And yes, as we arrived for our assigned visits, our arms were loaded with presents, not only for Jeremy but for Megan and her family as well.

It never ceased to amaze me that every time I would see Jeremy, he would reach for me, and I knew our bond was growing stronger and stronger. I thanked God (Yes, I was talking to God again) for that and the opportunity to be a part of his life. I was finally experiencing what a grandmother feels: complete fulfillment.

Chapter 19

It was your first Christmas. I texted Megan if I could send a Christmas stocking for you. She replied, "No, I'll get him his stocking."

I understood that, and it quickly reminded me that I had overstepped our tenuous boundaries. I sure wasn't going to do that again.

On that particular Christmas, we had the whole family visiting the farm for one of those over-the-top holiday celebrations. On Christmas Day, my niece Sara handed me a package. She's the eldest daughter of Katie, and she's one of those women…you know the type. She has four children and homeschools all of them. They are involved in outside the box programs such as fencing, medieval reenactments, and Shakespearean theatrical clubs. She makes all the costumes for these plays and reenactments by hand—there are no off-the-shelf purchases for this woman. She then proceeds to bake tasty treats for the after-parties, and in her spare time, she writes and edits a family newsletter for everyone's enjoyment.

Do I dislike her? Not in the least. In fact, I'm in awe of her talents, her dedication to her family, and her gift for appreciating everyone in her family—past, present, and future. Our family heritage is important to her. One of these traditions she continued was started by her great-grandmother—who is your great-great-grandmother, Jeremy.

Her name was Esther. Esther would knit Christmas stockings for every one of her grandchildren and great-grandchildren. Of course, Esther had passed decades ago, but Sara had found the pattern for Esther's Christmas stockings. And Sara, being Sara, had taught herself to knit just so she could continue the Christmas stocking tradition.

When Sara handed me the package, I was taken aback. I certainly wasn't expecting anything, but there it lay in my hands, wrapped beautifully in holiday-colored tissue paper, with a handmade card taped to the package.

I made the mistake of reading the card first. It was addressed to David and me, so I opened the envelope and began to read the first few words aloud: "I know it's hard not having Little Jeremy with you this Christmas…"

After glancing ahead at the next few words, I handed it over to David to finish. I just couldn't continue, because I knew that, in a matter of seconds, I would lose control of my emotions.

David took the note from my shaking hand and read the note out loud from the beginning. "I know it's hard not having Little Jeremy with you this Christmas, especially when you expected him to be with you every Christmas. I wanted to make this for him, so that whenever you do have him for a Christmas celebration, you'll have a family stocking for him. That way, you'll be able to continue the tradition of our family that his great-great-grandmother began. We all hope that in the future you will be able to fill it with wonderful goodies and Christmas memories to share with your grandson."

David glanced at me, his eyes welling up with tears. "Do you want to open it?" Not able to utter a single syllable at this point, I just shook my head back and forth. He gently pulled away the wrappings. Nestled underneath the red-and-green tissue paper was a red-and-white stocking, the same pattern that Esther had knitted for everyone in the family for decades! Your name was beautifully stitched into the top row. David handed me the Christmas stocking, and I clutched it to my chest, as if this action could somehow pull your essence into my soul and soothe my sadness. Yes, the wound of not having you with us was still very raw.

I glanced at David, and he just gave me that "Pull up your bootstraps and handle it" look. Do you think that worked? Nope. I felt myself lose control, as I fell back on the sofa in anguish, because I knew I would never have the opportunity to fill it for you or see your little face light up with joy at all the goodies and wonders that Christmas brings.

Everyone in the room was understandably silent. Katie came over to me. "I'm so sorry. I know Sara made this with all good intentions."

"I know." I sniffed. "It's just so unreal that this whole situation has turned out this way. And honestly, I'm not dealing with it very well." I hugged her, begged everyone in the room to accept my apologies for my meltdown, and excused myself.

I heard David saying to everyone as I left, "Mattie is having a really hard time with all of this. She just needs a bit of space to regroup."

Within a half hour, I was able to compose myself, and I ventured back to my family. I pulled Sara aside and said, "Sara, your intentions are wonderful and given from the heart. I am so sorry that my emotions got the best of me. This has been such a difficult journey for me and my family. I will cherish this stocking just like I cherish all of Esther's stockings she made for my family. Thank you for this precious and thoughtful gift. Maybe one Christmas I'll be able to fill it and give it to him."

Sara didn't say a thing. She just hugged me, and we cried together.

After Christmas, I put your stocking in a storage box, and to this day I have never been able to fill it with any Christmas goodies.

And then, just like that, your first birthday was just around the corner.

I can't believe I've written so much and for so long—and I've written it down in some sensible order. As I read over my musings, it still amazes me how horribly my family was treated. But, as they say, "What goes around comes around."

I wonder if one day karma will bite them in the ass. To this day, I'm still trying to figure out why karma continues to bite me in the ass! I know I've done some inappropriate and not-so-kind things in my life. But seriously, Lord: enough is enough!

I'm done writing for now, and I really need to go to sleep. Hopefully my sleep will be filled with good memories and not awful ones.

Chapter 20

I was beyond excited. It was the weekend of Jeremy's first birthday, and we were invited to attend his birthday celebration. Carole and my sister-in-law, Lauren, also wanted to come, so they had made arrangements to fly down and meet me there. Honestly, I was a bit nervous, since this was the first family get-together that we had been invited to attend. I hoped everything would go well and that Megan's family would be accepting and hospitable toward us. And that it would not be a repeat of the puppet master's previous encounters. The day of the party, I packed the car with all the presents adorned in blue paper and sparkling ribbons. Once again David opted not to attend, claiming that he needed to stay home with Poppa and take care of all the animals.

Thankfully, Claire was able to fly down a few days earlier so that she would be with me. Several weeks earlier, I had asked Megan if I could order a smash cake for the party, and she said that would be great. Let me tell you, that cake was a sight to behold. It, too, was carefully positioned among the birthday packages in the back of my SUV, waiting for Jeremy to enjoy it and smash it into bits and pieces.

Claire and I were excitedly talking about Jeremy's birthday. We were looking forward to meeting his other family members. Suddenly my phone vibrated with a text message. It was from Megan's mother. Since I was driving, I handed the phone to Claire for her to read it to me. I was thinking that it would say how excited they were to share in this wonderful occasion together.

But no, that's not what the text said.

Claire read the text silently, then cautiously looked over at me. "What's going on?" I asked. Without saying a thing, Claire put the phone down.

"For heaven's sake, Claire. Tell me what she said!" I exclaimed.

But as my daughter began to speak, I felt my heart fall deep into the pit of my belly. They had done it again… there was no birthday party with their family.

They were having a separate one for us, and we were to arrive no later than 3:00 p.m. and would have to leave by 5:00 p.m., before their family arrived. Once again, we were being told to leave.

I went from seventy miles per hour down to fifteen in mere seconds and pulled the car onto the shoulder of the freeway. I shut the car off and put the flashers on. Then I just sat there for a moment.

Now, Claire has seen me mad, but not this type of mad. After a moment of silence, I began cussing, and pounding the steering wheel with the ferocity of a caged animal. I truly could not comprehend the cruelty of these people and their continued ability to hurt my family. Claire simply remained silent, knowing to wait for me to finish my rant.

Finally exhausted, I hung my head in despair and disbelief. My carefully applied makeup had run in dark rivers of black from my latest meltdown. I looked like a clown, and I felt like one too—the clown that the whole audience laughs at for believing his other clown friend would not throw another pie in his face.

Surprise! I got another pie thrown in my face.

Claire reached her hand out to me in sympathy, but I just pushed it away. At that point, I wished my daughter wasn't with me in the car so I could just slam my vehicle into the next eighteen-wheeler that was passing next to my car and end all this anguish. I have a smash cake...why not have a smash car? Smash cake, smash car. Made sense to me at that moment. God, I was tired of all this.

Slowly I regained my sanity and reached for Claire, and we just held each other. Finally, I said, "Claire, I am so fucking pissed off! I just don't understand how a supposedly Christian family could do such unprincipled things to another family. And why are they doing it? My God, how do they sleep at night knowing that they have treated us like dirt? I just don't get it. It's not like we are uneducated, unprincipled, or anything. Both David's family and my family have ancestors that have done many historic things in the past. Jesus, David has an ancestor that was part of the first expedition to the North Pole. I have an ancestor that signed the Declaration of Independence for crying out loud. How can that be not good enough?"

"Mom, I know."

"No, you don't know, Claire. All these attacks are aimed directly at me."

"No, they're not, Mom."

Yes, they are, Claire. They blame me for Megan getting pregnant. They think that since I raised a son that wasn't using protection, all this is my fault."

"That's ridiculous. Megan was involved, too, you know."

"I know it's not logical, but that's how I feel."

"What do you want to do, Mom? Do you still want to go to the 'party?' Or go back home?"

"No. We will attend Jeremy's party. Your aunts are flying in."

Then I had another thought. "You know something? It just dawned on me that Megan's family had to have planned this 'birthday celebration' in advance and didn't have the courtesy or the honesty to let me know. That's just plain evil."

"Screw them," Claire said.

"Amen, sister. Amen. I need to call Carole."

I didn't bother to text Megan's mother. She did not deserve a response.

I punched my sister's number on my cell: no answer. Crap, they were still in flight, coming down to celebrate Jeremy's first birthday. Little did they know that we were not going to be allowed to attend the real family event. Just a fake one.

Glancing in the rear-view mirror, I wiped away what was left of my mascara, and merged the car back on to the interstate. As I drove due east, I realized that I had spent most of the past year crying about one thing or another because of our treatment from Megan and her family. It was only by God's good grace that Claire and I arrived at the hotel without issue. We checked in, went to our room, and put our luggage down along with the smash cake. Honestly, looking at the cake, it seemed to sit there, quietly begging me to smash the friggin' thing to smithereens! Megan had been so excited about me bringing it to the party. Now we had found out that there really wasn't a party for us anyway. We would be allowed a quick drive-by before the real birthday party took place.

I still had not received a return call from my sister. Because I couldn't warn them, I just started pacing in the hotel room, mumbling to myself. Claire watched me quietly. I felt like a caged, rabid animal, foaming at the mouth, ready to pounce on anyone or anything. I just couldn't get control of my anger that day.

As I continued to wear a path in the hotel-room carpeting, I started spouting off again to Claire.

"I have done everything according to their rules. I have shut my mouth, never pushing back on any of their directives. I just don't understand how they continue to behave this way!"

Besides being astute with animals, Claire was also in tune with humans, and she had always been a calming presence for me. She always knew when I needed a hug or a talk. And she was never intrusive. It was as if her genetic makeup were specifically geared to calm my Irish temper. And in that hotel room that day, she simply approached me in my anger, and as I allowed her to wrap her arms around me, she simply said, "Mom, we know that you have done everything the right way, the Christian way, and God also knows this. In fact, Megan's family knows this. No one can ever question your commitment or our families' love for Jeremy." I was astounded by my daughter's sage wisdom, and thankfully, after a few moments, I calmed down to a somewhat peaceful state of mind. Inside though, I was still boiling mad.

Claire and I busied ourselves by putting our belongings in the hotel drawers as we waited for my sister's and sister-in-law's arrival. Carole had called saying that they had landed, but I had decided not to tell them about the news over the phone. I didn't want them to hear this next bit of information while they were driving.

Carole and Lauren knocked on our door about twenty minutes later. They entered joyfully, but as soon as they saw Claire and me, their faces fell. Carole immediately came to me, and I collapsed into my sister's arms as I told her, through bouts of sobbing, the latest turn of events. Both women were absolutely dumbfounded by my news. Lauren, never one to back down, immediately stated that she would not attend the "private party." I completely understood her position and told her so, commenting that no one had ever treated any member of our family with such disregard and disrespect. As Lauren continued to pepper me with questions, Carole and Claire simply sat on either side of me on the bed, quietly supporting me. After answering Lauren to the best of my ability, I happened to glance at the time and realized that we needed to go to Megan's house soon so we wouldn't be late for our "private party."

When I mentioned this, Lauren again declined to go, stating she would never be a part of their calculating ways and went to her room. Although I had no control over the circumstances and it wasn't my fault, I felt ashamed and embarrassed.

Always there for me, Carole said she would come with us, and we all took a few moments to freshen up. As I washed my face and reapplied some makeup, what I saw in the bathroom mirror was an older woman, once again looking tired, broken, and lifeless. It was a person I did not know, and I didn't want to look at her image anymore. It frightened me. Turning away, I prayed for the stamina to make it through the next several hours without completely falling apart. It was Jeremy's first birthday, after all, and I had to be there for him.

We drove to Megan's house in utter silence. The beautiful birthday packages nestled in the back of the car that had brought me such joy hours earlier seemed bleak and listless now, just like me. We pulled into the driveway and, still without saying a word, we gathered all the gayly wrapped packages, and the smash cake and walked to the front door.

Pressing the doorbell, I wondered how I would be able to behave, and just as quickly as this thought passed through my mind, I felt my sister and my daughter's calming hands on my shoulders. I glanced over at

Carole, and she said, "We all love this little boy; it is *his* day. Let's enjoy it and not let anything else ruin the time we have with him." At that point, I don't think I could have loved or cherished any two people more.

The door opened. Megan and her mother welcomed us as if there was not a thing wrong with their decision. I must admit, they had prepared a lovely celebration table for us to enjoy, complete with balloons, cupcakes, cookies, and other baked goods. (By the way, it was all catered. There wasn't a homemade morsel to be had.) I knew the table was prepared specifically for the real party. They would just fill in what we had eaten after we left. I didn't partake at all.

We spent a wonderful two hours with Jeremy, opening presents and taking pictures. And then, just like that, Megan's mother informed us that we had to leave. Once again, we were told to leave.

Her announcement still hurt me, but at least I had those two hours that I will never ever forget.

Carole, Claire, and I showered Jeremy with hugs and kisses as we said our goodbyes. It seemed to me when I hugged him goodbye, he clung a bit tighter, as if his young mind knew that what was happening wasn't right and wasn't what he wanted. Maybe, it was just my wishful thinking.

Letting you go, I walked over to Megan, who had been hanging back in the corner of the living room, and just hugged her. She held on to me very tightly, just like her son, and in that instant, I knew she didn't like how we were being treated either. Unfortunately, I had yet to see Megan stand up to her mother, and it sure wasn't going to happen that day. I truly believe there weren't many people that would stand up to Megan's mother, in fear of the wrath that would surely befall them. I had been the recipient of it, and it wasn't nice.

We left your home before any of the "approved family" arrived. We were shooed out the front door and off the front steps to our vehicle as if we were door-to-door salesmen peddling cheap and unwanted goods.

As I pulled out of their driveway, I wondered if Megan's mother was hurriedly removing all our birthday gifts to Jeremy to another room. She most likely was, and she probably was spraying the whole house down with Lysol just to make sure any of our presence was removed completely!

We were not acceptable in their circle. It was a circle that included men dressed in seersucker jackets with bowties, shorts, and loafers with no socks. Their men had no calluses on their hands, and they sported names like Finn, Hayes, Reggie, and Winston, monikers that would be right out of a Margaret Mitchell novel, if she had ever written another. And the women partnered beautifully with their men. Their hair would be freshly highlighted and lowlighted from their weekly visits to the salon. Their nails would be buffed to a high sheen, and they would surely wear outfits from Prada or Gucci, with respectfully heeled summer sandals or platforms from the Charleston Shoe Company or Jimmy Choo, highlighting their respectfully manicured pink toenails. Honestly, it all reminded me of a Stepford community—they were all cut from the same cloth, with the same clothes, literally. There was not an individual among them.

The men and women in my collective family were all individuals.

I've already talked about Poppa and Mamaw, so I won't bore you by repeating myself.

My family was a mixture of individuals. My brother was the owner of a large business; my sister, Carole, was a retail buyer. My husband's side of the family included farmers, business owners, military men, and laborers.

So, obviously, in my extended family circle, individuality was allowed to shine.

More importantly, my family protected each member by supporting them emotionally and, yes, at times, financially.

I suppose that was what Megan's mother was doing. She was protecting her family like a mother lion. However, it was completely beyond my comprehension or any of my family's comprehension that she would deliberately hurt us for no obvious reason other than it was because we were individuals that didn't fit into their mold of what a "family" should look like.

Or it could be that if she accepted us into her family, then it would mean their family no longer fit her appropriate mold.

Chapter 21

As we left Megan's house, I turned to Carole in the front seat and uttered one word.

"Thanks."

Carole reached over and kissed me lightly on the cheek. "Mattie, we are all here to support you in any way we can. I know this is brutal for you. Shit, it's brutal for all of us, because we are having to watch our happy-go-lucky Mattie become a cynical and very sad woman. And truth be told, we miss you. But we understand why you are jumping through their invisible hoops. Jeremy's such a special little boy."

"He is special, isn't he?" I replied. "And Carole, the Mattie you knew is still here; she just has a few barnacles on her undercarriage!"

Carole sort of giggled and said, "So, is David going to be scraping barnacles off when you get back to the farm?"

Claire uttered a "Yuck" from the back seat as my sister and I went on a rant about barnacles that then turned into a joke about crustaceans and then finally about crabs.

By the time we got to the hotel, we were in hysterics with laughter.

Sister giggles were just what we needed.

Lauren joined us in our room once we returned. She wanted to hear every detail. Carole and Claire gave her the rundown as I remained silent. My jovial temperament from a few minutes before began to turn sour as my sister and daughter told Lauren the details.

Lauren was beside herself with indignation at their treatment of us. She began her tirade by exclaiming, "How dare they treat us this way? Do they not know who are family is? Do they not know our family's history? How in the hell can they think this is Christian behavior?"

We all nodded in agreement to Lauren's statements, and I did especially, since I had experienced it so many times over the last several years.

Carole sensed that I was not able to address the situation any further, so she said, "Lauren, none of us can understand the treatment that Mattie and her family have received from Megan and her family. All we can do is support Mattie now and in the future."

Damn, I love my sister.

I then spoke up and said to everyone in the room, "I really do appreciate each and every one of you and the support you have shown me, but I just can't rehash any more of this day right now. All I know is that I must continue to do what they demand so I can keep seeing my grandson. I can't lose him."

Then I lost my composure.

As these close women in my circle tried to console and comfort me, I realized that Megan's family's behavior and treatment of me and my family had just become too much for me to bear. I couldn't hold myself together anymore, and I didn't want to. I deserved a good cry.

I composed myself enough to thank everyone for their love and support but told them that I just really wanted to crawl into bed and try to sleep.

As Lauren and Carole left for their rooms, my sweet Claire crawled into bed with me. As she wrapped her arms around me, I thanked God for the love of my daughter and my family and drifted off to sleep.

I woke up early the next morning and went down for a cup of tea. As I sipped my tea, I called David about the latest drama. He listened to everything and simply said, "Do everything in your power to keep your relationship with Jeremy. I know you can do this."

"I could do it better if you were with me, David."

"You know I've got your back, Mattie, but you also know you don't want me there. I would ruin whatever tenuous bonds there are because of how mad I am with Jeremy's family."

"But I need you, David."

"Mattie, you've never needed me. You have always been your own person. I just taught you to embrace that person. You don't realize how strong you are. Just don't let other people dictate how you live."

"David, I don't feel strong at all. I'm tired of all the BS, and I'm tired of fighting this on my own."

"You're not alone, Mattie, I'm here for you. You should know that."

Honestly at that moment, it didn't feel like David was on board with me. He said all the right words, but his actions did not support those words.

We continued to talk about the situation, and things on the farm, and then we said goodbye. Claire was still sleeping, so I decided to hop in the shower for a hot, rejuvenating cleansing. I relished the sting of the water on my skin. To me, not only did the water clean my physical body, but it also cleansed my spiritual one. Feeling refreshed and now dressed, I noticed that I had received a text from Megan.

"Jesus, what now," I thought.

"My mom wants to take you and your family on a tour of our city. Can you be here by 10:00 a.m.?"

As I looked at her text, I shook my head, completely flabbergasted. These people didn't want us to be in their home to celebrate Jeremy's birthday, and now they wanted to act as tour guides! What the hell!

I didn't even respond to Megan's text.

When Claire woke up, I showed her the text. She was dumbfounded as well. "What do these people want from us?" she said. "They reject us one day and less than eighteen hours later they want to take us out on a tour. Don't they realize what they're doing to us? I don't get it!"

"Neither do I, Claire. But this is their typical behavior. One day we are accepted; the next we are rejected. I am only going to agree to this because we will get to see Jeremy again. As your father said to me on the phone this morning, I cannot let their actions dictate who I am. I must continue to be cordial and respectful so that I don't endanger our relationship with Jeremy."

Claire and I went down to meet Carole and Lauren for breakfast. As we sat down, I showed them Megan's text.

"This is absolutely absurd," Lauren exclaimed. "These people have no souls. Did you tell them to go screw themselves?"

"Lauren, you know I can't do that," I said. "Remember, playing by their rules keeps me in Jeremy's life."

"Well, this situation is beyond ridiculous. I'll go with you just so I can see what this other grandmother is all about," said Lauren.

With Lauren on board, I knew this could get extremely interesting! We arrived right on time, just like the puppets on a string that we were. Megan and her mother greeted us warmly, as if yesterday's behavior was no big deal. It wasn't a big deal to them, obviously, but it sure had left a permanent mark on us.

As we got everything and everyone situated in Megan's mother's car, she directed me to sit next to her. I politely declined, and looking straight into her eyes, I said, "No, I will sit next to my grandson." I did not back down as she continued to look at me, and she finally said, "That's fine."

"I'm so glad you think 'that's fine,'" I thought. "One thing's for sure. You sure as hell will not tell me where I can sit!" I just won another small victory.

We spent the day traveling around their city. And I must admit, Jeremy's grandmother was a fabulous tour guide and host. She was charming, knowledgeable, and funny as she showed us all the sights around her hometown. We all had a good time. Once again, I wondered if we were turning some invisible corner, traveling to a place where our two families could form a somewhat cordial relationship. But I had hoped for that too many times to put money on it.

After our tour, we stopped for lunch and enjoyed a very cordial meal. During lunch, I wondered whether she and I could have been friends if the situation had been different. But upon thinking about it...probably not. I had seen her true self at our first meeting, and subsequent encounters. I knew what I was now witnessing was a woman playing a role. Perhaps Megan asked her to be polite and charming. Or she was trying to impress Lauren. Who knows? But deep down, I knew this woman was all about protecting her social-standing in the community.

As we pulled into their driveway, she looked at me and asked if we would like to have Jeremy spend the night with us…Say what? I caught Carole's, Claire's and Lauren's looks of utter amazement. Of course, there wasn't any hesitation on my part. "Absolutely, we would love to spend more time with Jeremy."

Once again, there we were, gathering his things and bringing him back to spend time with his other family.

And wow, did we love it. Jeremy made us giggle and laugh as we crawled and played on the hotel room floor. (Well, Lauren didn't get on the floor, but she still had a grand time visiting with you.) And even though Aunt Carole was stressed about the dirty carpet, she, too, was down on that hotel floor playing with him.

What astounded me the most was that Jeremy didn't cry for Megan or his other grandmother. He was completely comfortable with us, his "unacceptable" family.

As Jeremy got sleepy, Carole and Lauren said good night. I settled him with a bottle and read him a book, just like I did for his father and his aunt Claire. As he drifted off to sleep, I continued to hold him and gaze at his beautiful face. I didn't want to let this baby boy out of my arms. Reluctantly, I laid him in the crib and thanked God for this day. Because just the night before, I was going to bed bawling, and now, twenty-four hours later, I was preparing for bed and gazing at my sleeping grandson.

I knew that I must take every good moment as it came and store them all away in my memory vault. There was no guarantee on how many memories I would be allowed.

The next morning, Claire and I packed Jeremy's things up and went downstairs with him to meet Carole and Lauren for breakfast.

Lauren asked to hold him, and as I passed him to her, she said, "I understand why you are agreeing with their demands. Jeremy is such a special little one, and he is completely in sync with you. He hasn't taken his eyes off you the entire weekend."

My emotions wanted to get the best of me after Lauren's statement, but I remained in control. I'd thought I was the only one who had noticed that Jeremy had always been looking for me over the last two days!

"Well, I knew before anyone in Megan's family that Jeremy was on the way. I was in constant contact with Megan during her pregnancy. And don't forget, Megan wanted me to adopt him. Jeremy knows me, and I hope he always will," I answered.

Lauren got up and handed him to me. As he settled into my arms, he turned toward me and wrapped his chubby arms around my neck.

"That baby boy loves you with all his heart, and he knows you love him just as much, or probably more. He knows he is part of you," Lauren said. With that, she left and headed up to her room to pack for her trip home.

"Oh, yes, he is," I thought as I watched her leave.

Within the next hour, Carole and Lauren left for the airport. Claire and I had everything packed and loaded up in the car to drop Jeremy off at his mom's house.

We arrived at his other grandmother's house and rang the doorbell. Within seconds, Megan's father opened the door. I had Jeremy in my arms, and as Claire brought all his belongings into the foyer, I handed him over to his grandfather. Immediately, Jeremy pushed at him with his chubby arms and turned toward me, reaching out and crying for me to take him back.

His grandfather's expression of hurt on his astonished face said it all: "Jeremy loves this woman. He barely sees her, but he knows her, and he wants to be with her."

At that moment it confirmed everything I knew in my heart. Jeremy loved me, he was connected to me, and he knew that I loved him unconditionally.

I did feel for his grandfather, but only just a wee bit.

We quickly said our goodbyes and headed back to the farm. As expected, it was another solemn car ride, but on the good side, we had gotten to spend time with our dear boy.

Chapter 22

Over the next year, we settled into the same approved arrangement as before, visiting Jeremy every month. Very often, Carole would join Claire and me for our visits. She would fly down, and we would pick her up from the airport, all of us giddy with the excitement of spending some time with Jeremy. Lauren declined from spending any more time with "those people," as she put it.

That was okay with me. I completely understood her feelings. But he wasn't her flesh and blood.

It was during this year that Megan met a young man: Greg was his name. He had a budding career, was from an established "Christian" southern family in which the men wore their seersucker suits, and the women were appropriately adorned according to the southern *Stepford Wives* protocol. (Yes, I'm referring to the women as being cut from the same pre-approved mold that was dictated by some unwritten rule.) He was actively involved in his church. Honestly, I was happy for Megan. She needed the stability and support that Greg could provide.

Sadly, my son was none of these things. I certainly wasn't angry with Ethan about this. He was his own free spirit, and he didn't conform to anyone's directive or prescribed attire, especially now that he had successfully completed USMC boot camp. Well, oddly, when I thought about it, he was now conforming to directives and clothing attire as prescribed by the US government. He had to follow the rules as dictated by the United States government. He had tested so high on the ASVAB (the Armed Services Vocational Aptitude Battery) that he was now studying cybersecurity. I was so proud of him for what he was trying to accomplish with his life. Somehow, because of all this turmoil, he had finally found direction and was getting his act together.

We weren't able to talk with him much while he was in school, but during one telephone conversation, I did ask if he had reached out to Megan regarding the military health insurance that was now available for his son.

"Yeah, Mom, I texted her about that. She told me in no uncertain terms that she didn't want the insurance, and she doesn't want me to ever contact her again."

Damn, that was harsh, but it didn't surprise me. I had seen the writing on the wall for a while, just by the previous lack of communication between Ethan and Megan regarding their son and how Ethan had already begun to distance himself from Megan and even from Jeremy. The girl that he had loved and had a baby with just didn't love him. I knew she never had.

I didn't know how to reply to Ethan other than to say, "I'm so sorry, son," and our conversation ended shortly thereafter.

I knew Ethan wasn't going to continue to reach out to Megan after her response to his text, and I didn't blame him one bit. Their relationship lasted just long enough for all his family to be entranced by its brief yet very strained beauty and for a child to be conceived. Unfortunately, we were all there to witness the last bloom of their relationship fall to the ground, brown, brittle, and dead. It reminded me of the decaying petals of the magnolia blooms that littered our lawn on a yearly basis.

Megan and Ethan were done.

Within two months of that conversation with Ethan, Megan and Greg became engaged. The announcement was even featured in their city's local magazine with a photo of them, for crying out loud! Megan had gotten her society engagement, while my son was left heartbroken. I honestly believed that he wanted to save their relationship, not just for Jeremy but because he did love his son's mom deeply. He'd tried to salvage it, but he just wasn't the type of man Megan needed.

After the announcement of your mother's engagement, I must admit this: I stalked them on social media. Mainly, it was with good intentions. I wanted to see that the man that would be raising Jeremy was okay. And thankfully, Greg seemed to truly love him and accept him. There were pictures of Jeremy with Greg smiling and holding him and Megan looking on, so I was happy to see that bond developing. I was of course very jealous of the pictures and also very wary of what this new relationship would do to my fragile visitation situation.

Thankfully, even as Megan and Greg prepared for their wedding, we were still allowed to visit every month.

My visits with Jeremy were my lifeline. He never ceased to amaze me, not only because of how sweet he was but because during every stay, there would be something he would do that reconfirmed our connection. It may have been a reach for my hand or a hug around my neck. Or a sweet kiss on my cheek. He would look to me for everything. It didn't matter if Claire was there, or Aunt Carole: he looked only to me for comfort, for play, for love. For whatever he needed, I was his go-to person. Aunt Carole and Claire saw it, as well, and often remarked on how in tune we were with each other. All these memories I stored deep in my heart so that I would never ever forget "us" and our unconditional and pure love for each other.

Chapter 23

It was just a few weeks before Megan's and Greg's wedding. All the showers had been held, and the gifts were collected and cataloged for future thank-you notes. Hair, nail, and makeup appointments were made. The caterer was busy with preparations, and the forecasted weather looked great. It was sure to be a lovely affair. And yes, ma'am, I found all this out by my social media sleuthing.

Although I knew full well that Greg was the right fit for Megan, I couldn't stop myself. It was stupid of me to follow Megan's social pages like I did, because witnessing their happiness unfold only wounded me more.

I talked to God a lot the week prior to the wedding. I prayed that the little boy that I called my own for a few moments in my life would be happy and content. I prayed that his mother truly loved this man. I worried about my son. And in a horribly narcissistic way, I worried about me. When was I going to heal and be myself again? Would this seeping wound ever heal? Would this constant unease ever cease?

Unfortunately, my invocations were not to be answered quickly. God was in control of His plan for me. Somehow, I had to be patient. But goodness, my patience was wearing thin.

I lost it the night before their wedding. It wasn't an "over the edge, lost all control" kind of thing, but it was a few hours of pure anger at the situation. David left me alone until I was ready for his support. For me, when my troubles are so intense, I need to sit, converse with myself, and find that quiet place to come to terms with what life has dealt me. It was on that night that I found myself on the front porch of the farmhouse, rocking in one of the two chairs that had been built over a hundred and fifty years ago from cedar trees located on the farm. The story goes that the chairs were built by Mamaw's great-great-uncle, who'd injured his leg during one of the Civil War skirmishes. It had to be amputated in one of the field hospitals known for their brutal surgical techniques. While he recuperated, he had carved his own wooden leg for the long walk home.

Arriving at the homestead, he'd felled the trees and built the rocking chairs that now graced the manor's front porch. The chairs were still in excellent condition after all these years, and the patina on the chairs was a beautiful gray that complimented the manor's field stone. As old as they were, you could still smell the cedar aroma, and they rocked smoothly back and forth as if they were on a cloud.

As I settled myself in one of the chairs, I thought about the hands that had built the chairs that night. They were the hands that, beyond unbearable circumstances, had succeeded in creating something beautiful. Those hands had endured a lot worse than what I was currently experiencing, that's for sure. That night, sitting there, I could almost sense my husband's ancestor as he worked the wood to and fro, making sure it was silky smooth to the touch. As I rocked, feeling the soft, warm wood beneath my hands, I came to the realization that I really had done everything right. I had supported Megan and Ethan. I had been there when they needed me from the very beginning. I had stepped up and agreed to adopt Jeremy. I had done nothing wrong.

So why was I continuing to torment myself over something that I had absolutely no control over? "When will I ever accept what happened and get on with my life?" I wondered.

David called me in for dinner, and we ate quietly. I was not in the mood for conversation that night. So, after dinner, and with the dishes cleaned and put away, I went back outside with a glass of wine (yes, I brought the whole bottle with me) to sit once again in the old rocking chair and ponder about everything I was unable to control. It certainly wasn't the smartest thing to do, but I did it anyway.

As I continued rocking and contemplating in the old wooden chair, the weather began to turn. A storm was brewing to the west, and the wind was beginning to whip the trees back and forth across the front pasture. I remained on the front porch, watching the storm escalate. The clouds moved and danced with the wind, building ominous thunderheads along the once vibrant sunset sky. The rumbles of thunder began, and the sound seemed to soothe my soul. It was as if Mother Nature's grumblings reflected the turmoil in my heart, resonating with the chaos that kept my mind and body from being at ease. The lightening shattering along the night sky was the percussion, the cicadas' noisy song was the string section, and the toads were the bass in my bizarre concert of nature.

I enjoyed it tremendously. It felt good to witness nature's anger because it reflected exactly what I was feeling. I was still angry. I had yet to accept what life had dealt me.

The rain was coming down in sheets now, yet I continued to sit in my chair with my wine. David left me alone. As I said, he knows me when I'm in that temper. Nothing will sooth me until I figure it out on my own. "What a perfect way to end this day," I thought to myself. Even nature knows and sympathizes with my anger.

As I watched the dance of light playing across the night sky, I poured myself another glass of wine, and then it finally dawned on me with the brilliance of a lightening flash that I was holding on to something in the past, something that I could never change. And just like that, I understood that I was the one tearing myself apart. My pain was simply a result of holding on to the past. I was not allowing myself to live and look forward to my future. I knew I had to make a conscious decision to get control of my life. I might not succeed, but I had to try.

I finished off my wine and as the storm continued to rage, I picked up my glass and the almost empty bottle of wine, walked back into the house, and headed to the kitchen, where I poured the remnants of the wine bottle down the sink. I went to bed that night with a new resolve.

When I awoke the next morning, the first thought that came to my mind was that it was Megan and Greg's wedding day. Oddly, I was okay. In fact, except for a slight headache from the wine the night before, I was great. It seemed as if overnight I had let go of all the hurt of the past several years and felt a tremendous sense of freedom. "Oh Lord, thank you for this healing! Sorry about all the wine, but I'm Irish!" I announced to Him as I got out of bed. Seriously, I had always been told that He was more forgiving of those with Irish heritage, probably because He knows we need more forgiveness due to our tempers and our love of spirits.

David greeted me cautiously that morning. "How are you doing?" he asked.

"David, I'm good. I feel great. That awful feeling of waiting for this day to happen is gone, and I can go on. I can't control their decisions; I can only control how I react to them. After breakfast, I'm going to write down what steps I need to take order to be the Mattie I used to be."

"What sort of steps are you thinking of?" he asked.

"Well, number one will be I will not live in the past anymore, wondering about what could have been or the what ifs. I will focus on looking forward to the future and the new adventures that await us."

"Okay, that sounds great. What's number two?"

"This one may be a bit difficult, but I am going to attend a small group study at Crossroads Church."

"What? Are you telling me you're going back to church? I have watched you over the past year fall to your knees nightly and praying to God for answers. Did He ever answer you?"

"That's not fair. Even though I've been very lax over the years, you know that my faith has always been important to me, so don't make fun of me. I'm thinking that as long as we don't receive any more horrible directives from Megan and her family, this small study group could help me. It's lessons from a book called *Forgiveness: Making Peace with the Past*, by Douglas Connelly, and it's going to be held on Tuesday nights at 6:00 p.m. starting next week at the church. Will you go with me?" I knew what his answer would be even before I asked, but I asked anyway.

"No, I'll pass. Anything else?"

I was a bit miffed at his response about the Bible study, so I asked, "Do you really want to hear it, or will you make a disparaging statement about this step too?"

"I'm not here to argue, Mattie. Tell me what you're thinking."

"All right. I think I'm going to start writing a journal. I'm not sure when I'll begin writing it, but I know one day I will find the time or find the need to clear all the negative memories out of my head by writing it down. I'm hoping it will be another way to heal."

David looked up from his breakfast and said, "I think that should be number one on your list."

"Really? Well, I don't have the time right now. I'll get to it eventually."

As I push back from the computer, I'm amazed at what I have written. I wonder how many other families have experienced this type of emotional journey involving a grandchild or a child. There must be millions of us out there that have been and are still pawns in another family's manipulations and mind games. Maybe there's a support group out there that I could join. Or, if not, perhaps I should start one. Because honestly, if you have never gone through it, you cannot explain the type of anguish you live with daily. I make a note to myself to research this later and briefly wonder if my story could help others. But the thought is fleeting, and I head to bed.

Chapter 24

The day continues. Megan was soon heading down the aisle to marry Greg and off to begin her life exactly as her family had hoped.

Ethan was overseas for twelve months serving in the Corps, and Claire had landed her dream veterinarian job and was beyond happy. As the weeks and months progressed, David and I continued our routine on the farm. And fortunately, during that time, I still visited Jeremy monthly. And then it happened.

Poppa died.

A few weeks prior, we had made the heart-breaking decision to move Poppa in an assisted living residence. Even with health-care aides coming in to assist us weekly, his care had become too much for us. It was a terrible conversation to have with Poppa, telling him that he could no longer live in his home. I wish we never had to have made that decision.

With Katie's approval, we placed David's father in an assisted living facility. It was lovely. He had his own suite, with a centrally located dining room and game room, as well as nursing and physical therapy staff on hand 24-7. But he didn't adjust well, and within two months we received a call in the wee hours of the morning. I heard the phone ring that morning and went out to the family room to find out who was calling at this ungodly hour. I found David, composed as he spoke to the other person on the phone. But as soon as he hung up, it seemed as if this were the last straw for him. His face collapsed, and tears flowed unrestrained.

"David, is it Poppa?" I asked.

He numbly nodded.

"Oh no! What happened? Is he okay?"

David shook his head. He was inconsolable.

As I sat next to him trying to give him some form of comfort, my thoughts drifted to Poppa. I loved him dearly. Over the last nine-plus years living with him, he had become more like a dad to me than my own father, (that was mainly because we had shared more personal and intimate moments than I had with my own father) and as the memories of him came to my mind, I grieved next to my husband. Our family had lost a loving patriarch. And with his passing, change would soon come to the manor.

Once it was a reasonable hour, David made the calls to his brother and sister that their father had passed. While he was doing that, I was on my cell calling other family members with the news. Then calls were made to the family lawyer and to Poppa's favorite pastor, to organize his funeral service.

Once all that was settled, I suggested to David that we have everyone over for a family conversation. There were several family members that wanted to keep the property and home, yet none of them would be able to dedicate their time or finances to the enormous upkeep that it required.

"That's a great idea. Let's wait until Katie arrives to have everyone over. She is so great at being a logical and calming voice in high-stress situations."

"When does she arrive?" I asked.

"I'm picking her up at 5:00 p.m. tomorrow, so let's plan for the next evening so everyone can come once they're finished with work. Would you be okay with making dinner for everyone?"

"Sure, I'll make my famous lasagna that Ethan likes so much. I wish he were here, though."

As I made the grocery list for my lasagna, I phoned my in-law's grandchildren and great-grandchildren that lived locally and invited them for a family dinner and a chat.

Katie arrived safely the next day, and as everyone gathered around Mamaw's dining room table for dinner that evening, Katie began the dinner with a simple request.

"Tonight, I want to do two things. First, I want to celebrate my dad's life by hearing memories from each one of you. That way we all get a chance to remember and honor the man we knew as Dad and as Poppa. Then we need to have a serious conversation as to what will happen with the house and the rest of the property. I am asking everyone to keep an open and logical mind as we discuss the latter situation, while we enjoy Mattie's delicious lasagna."

The next hour was filled with stories of Poppa and of Mamaw, as our family laughed, cried, and reminisced about both these wonderful people.

When I had finished serving the dessert, Katie said, "All right, I am going to open the discussion about the property and house with my opinion on what our future direction should be. I strongly believe that we should sell everything."

A chorus of no way erupted from the grandchildren and great-grandchildren.

"We love this place."

"I got married here."

"Where are we going to hunt?"

"I raised my children here."

David and I sat silently.

Katie listened and acknowledged everyone by simply stating, "I agree with each of you. We all have great memories here, and sad ones, too, but I'll now ask David a question. Although everything is paid for, David, my first question is, what is the yearly property tax on the manor and property?"

"Sis, last year we paid almost $40,000 in property tax on the house and the 475 acres (to put the acreage in perspective. It is about twice the total floor space of the Pentagon)."

There was stunned silence.

"David, so Poppa and Mamaw paid this every year?"

David replied, "Well, no. The last two years, Mattie and I have paid it because Mom and Dad didn't have the money."

With that statement, there was a litany of "Of course they had the money."

Katie interjected, "Everyone, please hear David out. Once he's finished, you can ask your questions. And by the way, no financial decisions regarding the property or my parents' finances were made without my approval."

With that statement, the dining room grew quiet again.

David continued, by saying "Their accounting firm screwed them. They thought that since Mom and Dad were older, they could get away with it. This is what they did. They took out numerous credit cards in Poppa's and Mamaw's names and would pay a bill with one credit card and then pay that bill with another credit card, only paying the minimum on the cards. The money they owed on credit cards was astronomical. None of you needed to know this, but now that it's out in the open: my parents were cash poor. As soon as I got down here and saw their financial mess, I fired the accounting firm. It has taken me seven years to get them completely out of debt. And to do so, Mattie and I purchased one of their commercial properties so that they would have cash flow. You guys have no idea the mess they were in financially."

Rachel, one of the grandchildren, now in her late thirties, looked at David accusingly and said, "Mamaw had a life insurance policy. I saw it on your desk. Where is that money?"

"First off, Rachel, I have a question for you. Why are you going through the documents on my desk?"

Katie immediately gave my husband a sidelong glance to dial it down a bit. But I too was wondering the same thing.

David caught the look and said, "I'm sorry. Mamaw did have paperwork for a policy. Thankfully she never signed it, because Mattie researched the policy while she was still alive and told her not to sign it. It was a scam."

"Oh. Well, what about the other commercial properties?" Rachel asked.

Apparently, she was going to be the mouthpiece for the group.

David calmly replied, "The other properties have been losing money for years. We will need to sell those as well. And, yes, before you ask, Mattie and I have been paying the taxes on those as well."

I was disheartened as I watched this conversation unfold. To me, as an outsider, it seemed all the family members around the dining room table besides Katie, David, and me were, number one, expecting that someone other than them would financially support the manor and its surrounding property so that it could remain in the family, and number two, they were wondering what the payout would be for them. They just didn't get it. There was no cash!

The grandchildren and great-grandchildren quietly talked among themselves about these new revelations.

Katie took this moment to ask, "Does anyone want to take over the financial and maintenance obligations of the manor?"

No one stepped up.

"If we sell it, can I still hunt here?" asked Matt, Rachel's husband.

"Really?" I thought. That was a question I didn't expect as I tried not to roll my eyes in bewilderment.

"I don't know," Katie replied curtly. "Any other questions?"

Rachel asked one more question, pointedly at David. "So, Uncle David, where did you get the money to buy Mamaw and Poppa's property?"

I could see David getting pissed at the audacity of her question, and at the same time I sensed movement under the table as Katie's short but powerful leg kicked her brother as a signal to behave. It didn't really work.

"Rachel, although it's none of your business, I'll tell you how Mattie and I were able to assist my parents, your grandparents, financially. We worked hard. We saved hard. We invested wisely, and that's what I would advise you to do with the money you'll receive when we sell this property. Anything else you want to ask me?"

And with that, the dinner was over.

Rachel and Matt left the table and went home.

The remaining family members helped clear the table and then peppered Katie and David with questions in the kitchen about what the property would sell for and what monetary amount they thought they would receive. It was one of the few occasions I relished doing the dishes!

Within the hour, everyone had left.

"Well, that could have gone better," I said.

Katie, always logical, said, "Actually, it went well. We now know exactly where everyone stands. No one is willing to step up and maintain or support the property, nor can they. It is a simple decision. We sell everything."

That evening, after Katie went to bed, I commended David on his handling of Rachel's questions.

"You did a great job with her, David. She can be overwhelming at times."

"Yeah, she can. And it took every bit of self-control not to tell her to mind her own business. I mean, really, how dare she ask me where we got the money! Are you ready to go home, Mattie, because I sure am."

"Well, I've been thinking."

"Oh crap, Mattie. What now?"

"Well, we love the white sands of the Florida Panhandle. What if we look for a house there? That way we will only be a few hours from Jeremy."

"Mattie, do you really want to look at houses down there?"

"Yes, David, I do."

But first things first, we had to get through Poppa's funeral. When the day of his memorial arrived, it was miserable, with torrential downpours. But the weather didn't stop the brilliant message from the pastor and the twenty-one-gun salute at the grave site. He went out with a bang—literally.

After his funeral, David was about to take Katie to the airport for her flight home. But before she got in the car, she turned to me and said, "You are one of the strongest women I have ever met, and I've met a lot. You were handed a huge challenge, and you accomplished it. You took care of my parents as if they were your own, and I will never ever forget the love that you gave them. You are an amazing woman."

Well, damn. Katie just made me feel like Wonder Woman! I had just done what any wife would do to support her husband. That's how I looked at it, anyway.

Finally, after a few weeks, everyone agreed that the farm should be put up for sale. After being on the market for about six months, we finally received an offer that the family accepted.

But before that, I asked David again if we could go down to the Gulf and look at houses.

"Why in the world do you want to do that?"

"I want a new adventure. I want a fresh life that doesn't smell of dead roadkill on the street in front of my driveway or have coyotes howling at night, or the fact that it takes me thirty minutes to get a gallon of milk! Never mind looking in my freezer and all I see is the family's kill of deer meat, turkey, or alligator! And don't even get me started about washing all the sweat soaked farm clothes or blood-stained hunting attire!"

"Was it that bad for you, Mattie?"

"Yeah, it was. I tried to tell you before we left that I didn't want to come down here. I only agreed because it was so important to you."

"Why didn't you tell me?"

Giving him a sideways glare, I said, "I told you, David, over and over. But you chose not to hear me. You were dead set on coming down here."

"I guess I was. I'm sorry. Have you talked to a Realtor?"

"I sure have, and all we have to do is call her."

"Go ahead and call her, Mattie. I owe you that much."

The next day, David and I were heading down to Florida. We spent the first night in Fairhope, Alabama, which is a lovely town. It reminded me a lot of Beaufort, South Carolina with the tree-lined streets and quaint shops. After dinner, I called the Realtor, and we confirmed a time to see three homes the next day. We had to leave early since Fairhope was quite a way from the Florida Panhandle.

Our Realtor was delightful and showed us two homes that were so-so. Then, the third one was it! It was surrounded by water oaks that had been sculpted by years of sea wind. The trees gave shade to a gray three-story shingled home that had front porches off each floor, each one offering a dappled view of the Gulf through the trees. Behind the house was a saltwater pool situated on a manmade canal that led directly to the Gulf of Mexico.

"David, isn't this beautiful? There's a pool, it's on a canal with a boat lift, and we can see the Gulf. I love it!"

"Mattie, I like the house too. But why are you trying to reinvent your life down here?"

"Dammit, David, it will keep me closer to Jeremy."

"Honey, it doesn't matter where you are. You will always be close to Jeremy. Whether you drive a few more hours or travel by air, you will always be there for him. Our house on the coast is waiting for us, and it's paid for. Do you really want to take out another mortgage at this stage in our lives?'

"Well, no, but I do love seeing the water. And our house in the Carolinas doesn't have a water view."

"I'll take you to the water anytime you want Mattie, and that's a promise."

After a moment of silence, I said, "David, I want to go home."

"Then let's go home, Mattie."

I thanked the Realtor for her time, and we got back in the car for our trip back to the manor.

But before we could really go home, the manor had to be emptied. Thankfully, Katie flew back down to help me with the daunting task of distributing items to family members. We spent weeks going through everything: dishes, books, furniture, clothing, kitchenware, artwork, jewelry, keepsakes, photo albums; it was an exhausting and emotional journey through the memories of two people that had been together for almost sixty years. Katie, now the matriarch of the Hill family, offered her guidance and suggestions during this process. Her presence eliminated any squabbles with relatives. Over the years that I had been down on the farm, Katie and I had formed a wonderful sisterly bond, and I was truly grateful that she was by my side during this emotional process.

By early spring, the farmhouse was void of everything, except what David and I were taking with us. The once grand rooms echoed with emptiness. The movers were coming the next day to load up our belongings and transport everything back east. The barn was empty; all the horses had been sold or moved to another barn.

As I walked through the vacant house and stables, I realized it was the end of a beautiful era for our family. No longer would we all get together to celebrate holidays around the big dining room table, host a wedding on the property, go on long trail rides in the woods, or wait to see what the hunters brought home from their endeavors. It saddened me to think about that time being over, because truly the house was filled with more good memories than bad.

I would forever have those memories.

Yet, I couldn't wait to get back to the life that I had so dearly missed for almost ten years, a life filled with less stress and more time for David and me to enjoy things together. Oh, and I wouldn't have to travel thirty miles to the nearest grocery store!

Chapter 25

Prior to us moving back to the coast, I still was able to visit Jeremy monthly. Most of the time, Aunt Carole and Aunt Claire would make time in their schedules to drive or fly down to meet me for our weekends. They loved spending time with him and building their own memories as much as I did. We would go on picnics and to children's museums, festivals, and playgrounds, all the while enjoying lots of dinosaur games, playing with Matchbox cars, and singing silly songs. Everything a grandmother and grandchild should do together.

Sometimes we would go to the local park. One memory I recall fondly was when Jeremy was just two years old and we were feeding the ducks in one of the parks while doing silly wiggles with our rear ends, mimicking the duck waddle. Aunt Carole was taking pictures of us as we wiggled and giggled. She could barely hold back her tears from laughing so hard. I love that memory.

Another time we were sitting across from each other for dinner, and I was smothering Jeremy in Nana-love, which I did on every visit. But on this occasion, once we had stopped laughing at how silly I was behaving, especially in public, he got up from his chair, walked up next to me, grabbed my face in his sweet, sticky hands, and kissed me on my cheek. As I write this now, I am a bit blubbery, not from sadness but from the pure joy that I felt from his childlike kiss. It was a gift of pure love given to me by my sweet Jeremy.

This memory is probably my favorite of them all: We had decided to go shopping at Target to find Jeremy a fun gift. Aunt Claire was pushing the cart, with him in the seat. I was right next to him, and as we walked down the aisle, he looked up at me, and without prompting grabbed my shirt and said, "You are my best friend."

The world stood still in that instance. I leaned down and smothered Jeremy with all the 'Nana love' I could give him. I never, ever wanted to leave that moment. I held on to Jeremy as if my life depended on it. And it did, actually. When I let go of him, I had to walk away to another aisle so that I could privately compose myself.

I knew Carole and Claire were looking at each other in complete bewilderment, because I saw their expressions as I walked away. "Why would a three-year-old child say such a thing to a woman he sees once a month? How is it possible that their relationship is that strong?"

I knew why. I was his grandmother, and he was my grandchild and shared an unbreakable attachment. Our connection had continued to grow, even though my time with him was so limited. I hoped neither time nor circumstances would ever sever that bond.

But, it would.

Chapter 26

Within six months of Poppa's passing, David and I had returned to our home in South Carolina, which we thankfully had not sold. It was a new beginning for David and me, and once the moving boxes were unpacked and everything put in its place, we quickly became involved in our neighborhood and community.

David was off to play golf—no more pastures for him to bushhog or fences to mend.

I reconnected with my old tennis friends and was playing weekly. I was very rusty but really enjoyed being out on the courts again.

Though I no longer owned any horses, I also decided I'd like to ride again. I reached out to Holly, who had been Claire's riding coach when she was younger. Holly still lived in the area, so when we finally connected, I told her I was back home and wondered if it would be okay if I exercised one of her horses.

"Of course you can, Mattie. It's so good to have you back in the area. How is Claire?"

"Thank you, Holly. Claire is doing great. She's finished her degree and is a vet in Virginia," I told her.

"I've seen some of Claire's posts on social media and knew she was doing well. That's great. How's Ethan?" Holly asked.

"He's fine. I have a grandson."

"Really? That's so wonderful. You've always wanted a grandchild."

"I have, but there's a lot more to the story that I'll tell you when I see you."

"Sounds good. You want to come out Friday and show me all the stuff the cowboys taught you down there?"

"I sure will, Holly. See you then. And thanks again."

I penned "riding with Holly" on my calendar. I couldn't wait for Friday.

I thrived being back home, reconnecting with my friends and neighbors, and getting involved in my favorite pastimes. All the miserable memories from the past several years somehow seemed softened by the happiness I felt being back where I belonged. Every morning, I relished each sunrise cresting over the tree line, erupting in a painter's palette of yellows, blues, pinks, and oranges. I went walking daily, breathing in the salty marsh air that seemed to fill my lungs with the promise of a renewed life. And I still got to see Jeremy! What could be better? Plus, to add to my happiness, Ethan was now engaged. He was completely over-the-moon in love with this young woman, and we loved her too. They were a good fit.

Our lives were back on track. At least for the moment, anyway.

The visits with our grandson were no longer every month because of the distance that we had to drive to get to Megan and Greg's new home in western North Carolina. But I was okay with that, because every visit was a chance to share more moments with him. Those trips were what I held on to…for dear life, because they were all I was allowed. I never experienced the weekly phone calls, the impromptu drop-in visits, the sharing of a holiday, or attending a school function or sports event. The visits were my lifeline to him, and I treasured each and every second of them.

I was now seeing Jeremy in the early spring and then again in the late summer. It became a routine for me to text Megan a month prior, and she would give me the dates that would work with her busy family schedule. I was always quick to confirm each visit.

One of our late summer visits was coming up soon, so I texted Jeremy's mom for dates that would work. She responded with the time frame, and I was so excited. I rented a house, and Great-Aunt Carole, Claire, David, and Great-Uncle Bob were all going to come, and it was for a five-day visit! I was beyond ecstatic. In fact, everyone was ecstatic! We eagerly planned for our week with Jeremy, looking up neat things to do and places to visit while we were there.

The house that I had rented was just a few miles from Megan's, so after I texted her that we had arrived, she pulled up a short time later. And there he was, smiling brilliantly at me through the car window. Oh, how that smile filled my heart!

Megan unloaded Jeremy's things, while Jeremy and I went into the house to say hello to everyone. Truthfully, I just wanted her to leave quickly so my family, his other family, could have him all to ourselves. As always, Jeremy easily adapted to everyone, never hesitating to play with David, Uncle Bob, Aunt Carole or Claire. And as always, he came to me when he was in need, whether it be for a quick snuggle, to play, to go to the bathroom, or get something to eat; it didn't matter, I was still his go-to person.

Our family spent the next five days thoroughly enjoying our time together. The days were filled with picnics, baseball practice with a big orange bat (just like his dad), walking the dogs, taking goofy pictures with each other, movies, and dancing barefoot in rain puddles, something I personally believe every child should experience.

In the evenings, when it was time for bed, I would read to Jeremy. I had done this on every single visit, from the time he was a newborn up until now, at five years old.

On the very last night of our visit, when I pulled out a book to read, Jeremy snuggled up close to me. I had only gone through a few sentences of the book when he suddenly pushed the book down, crawled even closer to me, and adamantly pointed at the ceiling, and clear as day said, "Can you see all the clouds up there and the lady that is smiling at me?"

I was a bit confused about his statement, so I gently asked some probing questions so I could better understand, like, "What does she look like? What is she wearing?"

He answered very distinctly that she had short curly white hair and a wrinkled face, was wearing a dress, and had a bit of red on her hand. I listened very carefully as he spoke, because I didn't want to miss anything. I asked if he had ever seen her before and whether she was nice, and he said, "Oh, yes, I've seen her before, and she's very nice. Most of the time I dream about her. But she looks old now, and she has that red stuff on her hand. Don't you see her, Nana?"

I certainly didn't see her, but I didn't want to inhibit his conversation, so I replied, "I do, sweet boy, I do," Satisfied with my response, Jeremy curled his body even tighter to me and fell instantly into a deep sleep while I lay there relishing in this beautiful yet rather unnerving moment with my grandson.

Does he have the gift of sight that no one is aware of? I wondered if Megan had witnessed anything like this from Jeremy. I also wondered if I should even ask her. She'd probably think I was loony. And who is this lady in the clouds? I wrestled with it for a good hour as he slept peacefully next to me. Eventually, I drifted off to sleep, still wondering who and what my grandson was seeing.

In the morning, I had totally forgotten about "the lady in the clouds" conversation. Megan was coming to pick Jeremy up in an hour, so we were all having our last breakfast together. I was sitting next to him as he ate his cereal, and just as calm as could be, Jeremy leaned over to me and whispered, "I'll always remember the lady in the clouds. I really like her."

No one else heard Jeremy's statement, and I was completely stunned by it. I leaned close to him and said, "I'm very glad that the lady in the clouds is nice, and I think she is looking after you. Always remember that your nana and the lady in clouds love you and will always be there for you."

Jeremy stopped eating, leaned over, and kissed me with milk-soddened lips and said, "I know."

Cleaning up the breakfast dishes, Carole asked me what the hushed conversation was between Jeremy and me. "Oh, we were just finishing up the story we started last night at bedtime, that's all," I replied. I didn't want to share that moment with anyone.

Right at the agreed upon time, Megan pulled up in the driveway. She handed me a beautifully wrapped gift, which I thanked her for. She seemed a bit more anxious and distant than when she had dropped you off, never fully making eye contact with me. I figured it was the fact that she was expecting her first child with Greg. But I did ask her, "Megan, are you okay?"

"I'm fine. I just have a lot of things to do today, and I need to get Jeremy home."

Wow, okay.

That was a bit blunt, but I put that thought aside as I buckled him up in his car seat, kissed and hugged him goodbye, and told him, "I'll see you soon. I love you forever."

I remember it like it was yesterday.

As he left the driveway, he never stopped looking at me as I waved goodbye and blew kisses, holding my gift. Another great visit filled with wonderful memories. Once in the house, I opened my gift. It was a beautiful set of figurines: a mother bird and a baby bird. "What a lovely gesture," I thought.

Little did I know it was my parting gift.

Tears are streaming down my face as I finish writing and reliving those last memories...my last memories of you. My fingers want to continue to write, but my heart is not capable of doing it anymore. It is so brutal knowing that tomorrow I will be writing the end of my story—no, our story, and my literary remembrances will be over.

I don't grab a bottle of wine as I leave my office. I grab a shot glass and a bottle of good old sipping whiskey from Kentucky that had been sitting in the bar for years, and head to the bedroom. I don't take any of my meds but throw back several shots as I watch reruns of Touched by an Angel. *Lady in the clouds.* Touched by an Angel. *How appropriate.*

Eventually, I pass out on top of my bed. My dreams are filled with you.

When I get up the next morning. I have a raging headache and fumble in the medicine cabinet for some aspirin. Gulping them down with the dregs of a shot of whiskey, I stumble to the kitchen, knowing I need good strong coffee and a full breakfast before I even attempt to finish my story.

I nearly burn myself cooking the bacon but somehow manage to make a good breakfast without sending myself to the emergency room. As I eat my breakfast and sip my coffee, my mind is full of the events of my last chapter and the ending of my story. My story would not be complete without this chapter but writing it down will be the end for me. Because this is when Megan's family completely shattered what was left of my spirit.

I know I must put on my big-girl granny panties to finish the final chapters, so after finishing my breakfast, I clean up the dishes, grab another big mug of steaming coffee, and head back to the office to write.

Chapter 27

I received a text from Megan about three months later stating that Greg now wanted to adopt Jeremy. They
wanted Ethan's contact information so that they could
send him the paperwork. I was floored! Before I sent
anything to Ethan, I texted Megan back to confirm
that my visitation rights would not be affected by the
adoption. Several days passed and she still had not replied, so I reached out to Jeremy's other grandmother
and asked her point-blank, "Will I still be able to visit
with my grandson if Ethan agrees to the adoption?" She
texted back almost immediately. Her text said, "Jeremy
loves his nana, and always will. You will always be a part
of his life."

After showing David the correspondence, we were both confident that we would still be a part of your life. I texted Ethan about Megan and Greg's request. He was adamantly against it. I reminded him that he had not been involved in his son's life for several years.

Ethan replied that he would take them to court, reminding me that Megan had stated adamantly four years ago that she wanted nothing to do with him.

"And do you really think you would win? Granted, you're overseas in the Middle East fighting for your country, because that is your job. However, you have not been involved with Jeremy for several years, even though you were told to stay away. You made no effort to fight for him. How do you think a judge will rule? It won't be for you," I texted.

It was brutal to write that, but it was the truth. I continued by saying that Megan's mother had assured me that even with the formal adoption, I "would always be a part of his life."

Several days passed before Ethan texted back and said simply, "Send me the paperwork."

Now, thinking back on the conversation with Megan's mother, I should have realized that she never said, "Yes, you will still be able to visit." She had only said, "You will always be a part of his life."

Chapter 28

It was a glorious day with little humidity, so I decided to work in the garden. The sky was that iridescent Carolina blue, with galloping wispy clouds that looked like horses' tails as they frolicked in midair. The hummingbirds had returned and were flittering about me, urgently requesting that I refill their bottles of nectar. I made note that I needed to get that done, but not before I finished pulling weeds and watering my garden bed of Shasta daisies and coneflowers, which the butterflies loved. My thoughts quickly went from the hummingbirds' needs to the fact that my next visit with Jeremy was coming up soon. I needed to text Megan to set up a time for the visit. Between the beautiful spring day and the idea of soon spending time with him, my heart was full of joy. I couldn't wait to hear his sweet voice say, "Hi, Nana." I was even more curious about hearing more of his imaginative stories about the lady in the clouds that he had told me on our previous visit. To this day, I've never told anyone about our cloud-lady conversation. I wonder why I had kept it private. Perhaps because it was just that: a private moment between myself and my grandson. Keeping it to myself meant that it was completely our moment.

I had approached David several days ago about renting a house again for our next visit with Jeremy. He was all for it, since everyone had such a wonderful time the last time.

Taking a break from working in the yard, I texted Megan, inquiring about a good date for our semiannual trip. I was not expecting an immediate response, because she normally would reply in a day or two. I went back to my business in the garden and finally fed those demanding hummingbirds.

I didn't hear from her in a couple of days. I didn't hear from her in a week. I texted several times, inquiring about our visit, and it showed that my texts had been delivered. Obviously, she hadn't blocked me; why would she? But why hadn't she responded?

This new behavior from Megan brought up the same old question: "What game is that family playing now?"

I really began to stress about the situation, so I asked David what I should do. He said, "Give her some time. She's busy with the new baby; she'll get back with you."

"I've given her almost two weeks now to reply. What could have happened that she wouldn't respond?" I exclaimed. "I hope there's nothing wrong with the new baby."

"Wait a few more days; she'll get back to you," he said.

Taking David's advice, I continued through the next couple of days, doing my errands, volunteering, playing tennis, and horseback riding. Unfortunately, no matter how busy I kept myself, I was unsettled.

I have often said to David that I have an uncanny ability to sense when things are not right with my family and loved ones. He laughs at me and tells me that I'm ridiculous. But if I were a betting person, I'd be in Vegas and do very well due to my percentage of accuracy. And at that time my intuitive Spidey-sense (which I call it) was tingling off the charts! I had to do it: I texted once more. And once more I did not get a reply.

Thinking I needed to clear my head and get a new perspective on the situation, I drove down to our local

park, by the river's edge, and gazed out across the sparkling water, hoping the beauty that surrounded me and
the chattering of the shorebirds would ease my unrest.
It didn't.

I couldn't understand this turnaround behavior.
Jeremy's mom had always been communicative with
me, sending me pictures and gifts, thanking me for gifts
that I sent for him and her, sending cards: always acknowledging that I was your grandmother. And now,
nothing. How could that be? What could be wrong?
What the hell has happened?

Not finding any peace or direction, I decided to walk
downtown. It brought me some solace, as I greeted familiar faces and enjoyed the beauty of our quaint little
town. As I neared the local children's boutique and gazed
at the toys on display in the windows, I thought about
the times that I had delighted in going in and purchasing
things for Jeremy: that Halloween costume, the bedtime
book or the funny dinosaur puppet that he so dearly
loved. I passed the ice cream shop where I had taken him
with Aunt Carole. I remembered that Jeremy was more
enamored by the train running around the top of the
room than the bowl of ice cream sitting in front of him.
(It didn't go to waste: Aunt Carole and I finished it off!)

As I continued my walk, I knew I couldn't be a part of this game-playing anymore I felt as if I were the unsuspecting victim stuck in some vicious loop of the old series *The Twilight Zone*: existing in an unknown dimension, with no way to get back to reality. I needed an answer.

I sat down on a bench along a beautiful brick passage, with crape myrtles that created a complete canopy of shade over the walkway thinking, "Lord, give me strength." Almost instantly I was given the answer. "I need to reach out to your other grandmother." I thanked the Lord for his insight, and with my mind set on the direction I should take, I texted Jeremy's other grandmother, asking if everything was okay with his mom and the new baby, and noting that I was concerned since I hadn't heard anything about our next visit. I received an immediate reply from her stating that everyone was fine. But no answer regarding my visit.

She hadn't answered my question, and now I was really pissed off! I was completely unnerved that my relationship with Jeremy could be in jeopardy. I needed to talk to David. I hurried back to where my car was parked and announced out loud to no one in particular, "They promised me." Somehow, saying it out loud solidified it as being the truth. As I reached my car, my cell rang, and it was David. David is not one to use his cell phone regularly, only for matters of urgency, so I picked up immediately and with concern asked, "Is everything okay?"

"Mattie," he said. "We received a letter from Megan's mother."

"Okay. Read it to me," I replied as I buckled myself into the car. David hesitated and then began to read the letter.

I felt my world begin to go black and cold as I listened to David's voice.

Mr. and Mrs. Hill,

Upon the legal adoption of Jeremy Crawford Hill by my husband, Greg Dawson, your rights as grandparents have legally been severed as of the date of the signed adoption. It is the law in the state we live in that since you are the parents of the biological parent that gave up his rights, then you as well have lost your rights to be a part of Jeremy's life. This means that you will have no future communication of any kind with Jeremy or our family.

We do wish Ethan all the best with his future bride.
God bless you and your family.

Denise Cunningham

I said nothing while David read the letter. I couldn't.
My mind wasn't comprehending the words David had
read to me. I had been promised that I would always be
a part of Jeremy's life, and then in a moment of clarity, it
hit me like a lightning bolt. Megan's mother's text didn't
say I would still be able to see him. She had just said that
I "would always be a part of" his life.

Then I thought, "How dare you sign it 'God bless
you and your family'? Jeremy is my family! You lied,
and you broke your promise—again! You've taken my
Jeremy from me!"

In a fog, I heard David's voice: "Mattie, did you hear
me? Are you okay?"

"I heard you, David. I'll be home in a few minutes," I
said, and ended the call.

In a blur, I started to drive home. I desperately tried
to hold back tears, but to no avail. It was nearly impossible for me to focus on driving as I tried to see through
the torrent of tears cascading down my face. Thankfully,

in an instant of sanity, I knew I shouldn't be driving, so I pulled off onto the shoulder of the highway and turned the car off.

And then, it just happened. All the sorrow, the manipulation, the pain that I had been trying to manage and to hold somewhat at bay for the last five years erupted out of me with a howl. I couldn't believe the sound that poured from me like a wounded animal. I can still hear that sound, all these years later. If you've ever heard coyotes screaming at night, that's what I sounded like. Weeping, screaming, and cursing all at the same time brought nothing to ease the agony as a black veil of hopelessness overwhelmed me. I felt nothing, just an overwhelming emptiness. I was sure my soul had died and shriveled into nothingness from this wicked decision. Wrapping my arms around myself, trying to ward off this horrible feeling of abandonment, I rocked and prayed for understanding and solace as I sat in my car on the edge of the highway. It didn't come. Someone I dearly loved had been taken from me, and I was dead inside. I was still breathing, but I was completely broken, spiritually and mentally, and completely lifeless. They had finally broken me.

With the traffic roaring past, I opened my car door and proceeded to vomit uncontrollably on the side of the highway. It was as if my body needed to purge itself of all the ugliness that it had been harboring over the last several years.

I heard my cell ring, and, reaching for napkins, tissues, anything to clean myself up, I answered. Of course, it was David. "Where are you? You should have been home ten minutes ago," he said.

"I couldn't drive, David. I lost it! I think I'm okay now," I answered.

"Do you want me to come and get you?" he asked.

"No, I can make it. I'll see you soon."

Thankfully I made it home. I walked into my house in a fog and collapsed in David's arms. David just held me for hours as I wept and screamed and cursed all over again. This was a pain that was physical, emotional, and spiritual. And it was all because of a decision made by another family. They placed a piece of paper with somewhat legal jargon in a stamped envelope and informed me that, again, I was not good enough.

I had lost my grandchild.

David eventually coaxed me to lie down in bed. As I curled up in a fetal position, he lay down next to me, cocooning me in his love and held me until around 4:00 a.m., when I finally fell asleep, completely and utterly exhausted.

I'm finished writing for now. I've been working on this "journal" for months and months. I really didn't want to write this part of the story. It doesn't matter that those memories are over a decade old; they are still raw for me. I think it's time for a glass of wine, just a small one, before I continue with the rest of my story, 'cause it ain't over in my mind. "Maybe it's a good time to take a break from writing," I think. "This process has worn me out completely, and I need to remove myself from it before my family commits me!" I then decide I need to call the kids and let them know what I'm doing. I grab my phone and text Ethan and Claire, telling them I would like to talk to them tomorrow and will call them once they're home from work. Claire immediately texts back: "Are you okay, Mom?" I reply, saying, "Yes, I'm fine. I'll talk to you both tomorrow."

At 6:00 p.m. the next evening, I FaceTimed with both my children.

"Hey, guys, how are you both doing?"

Ethan replied first. "I'm great. I just finished a big networking job at a corporate bank, and it looks like I might be up for a promotion next quarter."

"That's fabulous, son. I'm so proud of you. Claire, what's going on with you?"

"It's been super busy at the clinic. Yesterday I had to work on a dog that had a prolapsed uterus."

"That's disgusting, Claire," Ethan piped. "I don't know how you do that kind of work."

"Well, I don't know how you work on switches, motherboards, and all those inanimate objects every day. Where's the satisfaction in that?"

As they began to bicker in that friendly manner that siblings do, I interrupted their dialogue.

"Both of you, stop talking. I have something to tell you."

"What is it, Mom? Are you sick?" they both asked.

"I'm fine, guys. Just listen to me for a second. I have started writing my story. And I wanted to make sure you both are okay with that."

"What story, Mom?" Ethan asked.

"Geez, Ethan, don't you know anything? Mom's writing a story about Jeremy," Claire said.

Claire knows me so well.

"Mom are you really writing a story about Jeremy?" said Ethan.

"Well…it's more like a journal of what happened to us as a family, and more specifically how it affected my life."

"But why are you writing it, Mom?"

Claire jumped in and answered for me. "Ethan, don't you get it? Writing her story is helping Mom get all those bad memories out of her head and helping her heal. Communicating her thoughts on paper enables Mom to find her voice again. Isn't that right, Mom?"

"Well, yes," I answered, thinking Claire had hit the nail right on the head. "But it also brings it all back to the forefront and at times really exhausts me and gets me pissed off all over again."

"I'm sure," Claire stated.

"So, are you guys okay with this?" I asked.

"I'm okay with it," Ethan said. "It's not like you're going to publish it as a book."

"No, that's not my plan. Claire, are you okay with this?"

"Sure. Whatever helps you heal, Mom."

"Well, I feel better just telling you both what I'm doing. I'll send it to you once I'm done."

"Sounds fine to me," Ethan said.

"Me too," Claire echoed.

After a few more minutes of idle chatter, we disconnected.

I was glad I'd told them. It wasn't a secret anymore.

I knew I would be ready to write again in a week or so.

Chapter 29

After a few hours' sleep, I woke up. I looked over, and David was still there, awake. "Why are you awake?" I asked.

"I needed to stay awake in case you needed me. Are you okay?"

I have never loved David more than that moment. He had stayed awake the entire night because he knew that I was on the very fragile edge of insanity.

"No, I'm not okay. But I really need to go to the bathroom. What time is it?"

"It's around nine thirty in the morning. I'm going to make some coffee and breakfast. Do you want some eggs and bacon?" he asked.

I didn't reply; I just went to the bathroom, relieved myself, and looked at the woman in the mirror. I stared at an image of a person with puffy, bloodshot eyes and a face that had aged ten years over the last twenty-four hours. "That can't be me," I said out loud. But it was. I quickly looked away. I didn't want to see this person. Once again, a shell of what she had been. A woman that was a grandmother, and now was not.

David hollered from the kitchen. "Your breakfast is ready."

"I don't want any," I replied.

"You have to eat."

"No, I don't. In fact, I want a drink!" I told him in no uncertain terms.

"Mattie, it's only 10:00 a.m. You don't want to start drinking now."

"Yes, I do, because I really don't give a damn what you think, or what anyone else thinks. I need to dull this pain somehow, and a drink sounds good to me."

He gave me a stern look of disapproval as I walked over to the bar, made myself a tall Bloody Mary, and called Carole.

Carole picked up almost immediately. As I sipped my cocktail, I started crying again, telling her what had transpired over the last twenty-four hours. We wept together at the injustice of it all. After about forty minutes of conversation, Carole asked, "So, what are you going to do?"

"What do you mean, what am I going to do? What can I do?" I replied briskly. "They blatantly told me I have no rights."

Carole replied, "Well, don't you think contacting a lawyer might be a good idea to confirm that? You have all those gifts, and cards from Megan, as well as all the photos of visits to verify that you and your family were allowed to visit with Jeremy. Surely that should mean something in court."

By this time, I was on my second Bloody Mary and just replied, "I'll think about it."

We talked for another good hour, and as we said our goodbyes, I thanked her for always being there for me through the last five years.

"You never have to thank me, Mattie. You are my sister. I am here for you, just as you've been there for me. We are family, and I love you dearly. Just think about contacting a lawyer, okay?"

I always felt better after talking with my sister. Throwing the rest of my drink in the sink, I went back to bed.

I slept through the rest of the day and the entire night. When I woke up the next morning, I had a new purpose.

I realized Carole was right. I had to fight this. Not doing anything was giving in to them, and I was not going to do that.

As I readied myself for the next challenge in this battle, Helen Reddy's song came to my mind: "I am strong. I am invincible. I am woman!"

I got this. I was going to hire a lawyer.

I told David what my plan was, and he said, "Go for it."

"It could get expensive," I said.

"That doesn't matter. You do what you need to do to fight for our grandchild. I'll support you."

"Okay, I'm going to make some phone calls."

So once again I began to search for a lawyer. I needed to find one that was near Jeremy's location yet not affiliated with their hometown. They had a lot of connections. I had to be sneaky, just like they had been.

I reached out to one law firm and left a message briefly outlining my situation. The paralegal called me back within the hour. We spoke for almost an hour, and she said, "Mr. Talbot would be very interested in representing you."

I hung up, overjoyed, and relayed the information to David.

"All is not lost. I can fight this. I can certainly win the right to see you again," I thought.

We sent the retainer to Mr. Talbot to secure his services.

Mr. Talbot spent several weeks researching our options, and when he called me, he confirmed that I had no rights in the state where Jeremy resided. If we were to pursue it, and hope beyond hope to win after a lengthy court battle, our visitations would be governed by a court-appointed representative in a cold, sterile room inside the courthouse.

No, that is not what I wanted to do to my grandson.

I declined that option, yet still not wanting to give up, I asked him, "What if I compose a letter, acknowledging that we understand about the cessation of our legal visitation rights as grandparents, but because of our history over the past five years, ask whether it would be acceptable if I would be allowed to communicate with Jeremy, not as a grandmother per se, but as 'Aunt Mattie.'"

I thought this may be a great solution to a very horrible situation.

He stated, "It's worth a try."

It took me days to compose the letter to my satisfaction. I sent the draft off to Mr. Talbot's office, and Janet, the paralegal, called me back with a few edits and suggested that once the edits were done, to send a copy to their office and send certified copies to Megan, Greg, and Megan's mother. That way one of the three would surely sign for it, and we would have acknowledgment that it had been received.

The next day, I was in the post office sending out my certified letters, praying that my urgent request would be acknowledged, understood, and accepted.

I had sent the letters on a Thursday, and I still hadn't heard anything back from Talbot's office by the following Tuesday, so I reached out to Janet, wondering if she had received any response from my letter. "No, nothing yet," she said. "That could be a good thing."

Taking that statement to heart, I felt like things were going to change for the better.

That following Thursday, Janet called me and told me they had received a letter from their lawyers.

As she read their response, I knew we had lost.

Mr. and Mrs. Hill,

The Dawson family believes that it is in the best interest of Jeremy Dawson's welfare not to have any communications with you or any member of your family now or in the future. They only want what is best for their child.

If you ever contact any member of the family again, their only recourse would be to take legal action against you.

Sincerely,
Joshua Black
Black and Coffey
Attorneys at Law

Completely bewildered by this statement, I said, "Janet, they have no grounds to send such an outrageous letter. We've done nothing but support Megan over the last five years. Is there anything we can do?"

"No, Mrs. Hill, there is nothing you can do."

I simply said, "Thank you for your time. Please send me a copy of that letter," and ended the call.

On that day, as the sun shone brightly outside and the crisp sea breeze rippled my curtains through the open window, I sat stunned, knowing that I had lost Jeremy forever.

I found David and told him the news. "Are you okay?" he asked.

"No, I am not fucking okay, and don't ever ask me that again," I yelled at him. "I will never be okay, ever again. Don't you understand that?"

I saw how hurt he was at my reaction, but it didn't matter to me at the time. I was beyond caring for anything or anyone. And he knew once again to leave me alone.

I went to the outside refrigerator, grabbed a bottle of wine and a glass, and went outside to drown my sorrows. Sitting outside on the back deck, I couldn't even cry anymore. I just sat, drank my wine, and had major conversations with the good Lord.

Chapter 30

The next morning when I saw David, I grabbed him and hugged him hard. "I am so sorry I took everything out on you last night. Please forgive me," I said.

"Mattie, I forgive you, but this has gone on for way too long. You're killing yourself and us over this. You must let it go."

I was taken aback by David's statement.

How could I let it go?

I knew David supported me, but he didn't understand my loss. Dammit, it was our loss, but he didn't feel it as an attack to his soul, like I did. Yesterday we were told once again that we were not worthy of being grandparents. So how, I ask you, do you look in the mirror the next day, or the day after, knowing that another family thought you and your family were unworthy of the greatest gift of all?

"David, how can you ask me to let it go?"

"Because you are becoming a raging lunatic, as well as drinking way too much. You're killing yourself over this, and your only focus is Jeremy. What about us, dammit?"

Angrily I replied, "Of course my focus is on Jeremy. He's *our* grandchild, not just mine. Why don't you focus on him with me? Why do you always say you support me, yet do nothing to support me? Actions are stronger than words, David."

Glaring at me, David left the room.

That night I wept alone in our bed. David had gone to bed in the guest room. He didn't want or know how to be there for me anymore.

I wept for that part of my soul that believed people inherently do the right thing. I wept for the child that had been taken from me. I wept for all the promises broken. I wept for myself. Later that night, after David was asleep, I went from room to room in the house, quietly removing Jeremy's pictures and any gifts that Megan had sent me. I pulled down the sign that read "Nana and Grandpa's House." Every hat, bag, or shirt that said

"Nana" or anything regarding being a grandparent got packed up in a Tupperware box and put in the attic. I just couldn't bear to look at all the reminders anymore.

I did not put away the mother bird and the baby bird. Oddly, it felt important not to pack them away.

The days turned into weeks and then into months, with no relief from the anger and feelings of betrayal. I dreaded waking up in the morning because anger and sadness was all that greeted me as each day broke. Somehow, once again, I soldiered on. I went through the motions of daily living. I walked the dogs and visited neighbors, talked with my sister; but always right there in the forefront was my anger and hopelessness. Only my family and a few of my close friends knew what had happened. They would often check in on me and ask how I was doing. I simply replied, "I'm okay. I'm here."

I began leaving a light on in the bedroom when I went to bed. I had to have some sort of light, because I had become afraid of the dark. Not the dark of night, but the pitch-black darkness that I lived in now. I had become so fearful that when I did sleep, the darkness would completely envelop and absorb any part of me that was still left, leaving behind a dark hollow shell of a human being. It was the absolute darkness of betrayal and death.

I felt dead. I mourned not only the loss of my grandson but also the loss of myself.

I did try to heal. I went to church. I read self-help books; I went to a therapist. I worked in the garden with a newfound frenzy. I found some solace in digging in the rich, dark soil. In fact, I felt closer to sanity when I was digging in the garden than at any other time. I felt connected to something—Mother Earth, nature, God. Who knows?

I weeded, planted, mowed, and trimmed. I planted a garden for Jeremy, hoping that when the spring blossoms budded, I would find joy. They bloomed, and I weeded around them, but all I had from this endeavor was calloused hands, broken nails and little joy. I didn't have Jeremy in my life, just lots of new flowers from his garden that sat in vases in the house.

It had been a year since the "decision," and I continued to function on a somewhat normal level—or so I'd thought, until David had a come-to-Jesus conversation with me one evening on the back deck. He made me aware that I was not functioning normally at all and that I needed to do something about this issue, and quickly!

He simply said, "Mattie, I was wrong to tell you to let it go. Don't let it go. I think what you need to do is take what has happened to you and our family and embrace it. Take this experience and figure out how you can make the new you something you would be proud of. You're still in there, Mattie. Find you again and become an even stronger woman than you already are. I need you to come back to me. Your family needs you to come back."

Well, damn, David!

I wept in his arms, not out of sorrow but out of gratitude that he had found the words to begin breaking the wall of darkness that had encased me for the past year.

I was determined to find me again, but it was going to be an enormous challenge.

I went for long walks, looking for answers, and found some solace in the beauty of the parks in our area. I brought my old camera out, sat on benches, and took lots of photos of living things, beautiful things, that through my camera's eye showed me once again the magnificence and purity of life. And, just like that, while enjoying God's glory surrounding me, I understood what I needed to do—I needed to forgive. If I could forgive those that had caused me this pain, I had hope that my pain would end.

I made the decision to forgive. I prayed fervently to the good Lord to take my anger away and give me grace to forgive. Honestly, it took a bit longer than I had hoped, but one morning it happened. I still see it clearly in my mind. I woke up extremely early, somewhere around 2:30 a.m., and decided I wanted to sit out back, in the garden. The night air was still a bit sultry, but it had the soft kiss of cooler weather coming soon. I listened to the conversations of the owls as they hooted back and forth and reflected on the shambles that my life had become. But then, suddenly, I was able to let myself remember all those wonderful memories of Jeremy. As the frogs and night creatures chattered in the background, I realized that I could no longer ignore those memories. Our memories will keep me alive. I have a grandchild, and I have memories to prove it. I have pictures and shirts, hats, and gifts from him.

I felt so much lighter. I turned my eyes to the night sky, smiling, and watched as a shooting star raced across the sky. It was a sign, and I felt the beginnings of forgiveness.

That night, I brought all Jeremy's pictures back out and placed them lovingly among my other family pictures. His photos sat nestled between his great-grandparents and next to his aunts and uncles. My last picture of Jeremy was placed right on my bedside table so I could say good night and good morning to him every day.

Chapter 31

With renewed purpose, I was able to get back to living. I began volunteering at a preschool for special-needs children. I joined a book club and played cards with the girls at the club. I was finding the new Mattie, and it felt good.

Plus, Ethan and his fiancée, Morgan, had set a date for their wedding. So, I had that to look forward to.

One of my neighbors called one day and asked if David and I would like to chair the social committee for our neighborhood. I was completely honored and a bit flabbergasted that she would ask us and told her so. She simply replied, "Mattie, you and David are always so courteous to everyone, and you both have that southern charm that is so welcoming. And, from what I hear, you can throw down a great party."

"Well, thank you, but I have to check with David before we can commit to cochairing," I replied.

I hung up after we chatted for a few more minutes about the responsibilities of the committee. And then I went to find David to ask him what his thoughts were on this new challenge.

I went outside to find him because he had been cutting the yard just a few minutes before. As I hollered for him out front, my mind briefly acknowledged that it was odd that I didn't hear the lawn mower running. Walking around back, I saw David sitting on the mower that wasn't running in the side yard. His back was toward me.

"David," I yelled. He didn't answer. "Damn it, I wish he would wear his hearing aids," I thought.

"David, answer me," I hollered again.

It was then that I knew something was very wrong. David was not moving. My heart was pounding out of my chest as I ran toward David. As I got closer, I noticed that his head was slumped forward. Thankfully, I had my cell on me and dialed 911. I had just reached the back of the lawn mower as the operator answered: "911, what is your emergency?"

I walked to the front of the lawn mower and saw my David. A smile was on his face, but his eyes were open and glazed.

"Noooo," I wailed as I dropped my phone, trying to find a pulse on David's neck. There wasn't one.

I heard the 911 operator still trying to communicate with me as I climbed onto the lawn mower and wrapped my arms around him.

"You can't leave me, not now. What am I supposed to do without you?" I screamed.

"Ma'am, please tell me your emergency."

Somehow, I regained enough composure to reach down and grab my phone. "It's my husband. He's not breathing. He's on the lawn mower in our side yard. Oh, Jesus, please help."

"Ma'am, can you find a pulse?"

"No. His eyes are glassy and fixed."

I didn't hear another word the 911 operator said.

I sat on the lawn mower, holding him and weeping. I had no idea how long I sat with him. It could have been minutes, or even seconds, or an hour. I just knew David was gone.

I heard the sirens and vehicles pulling into our driveway. I heard the voices of our neighbors next to us, who had come over after they had heard my screams. I heard the gurney rumble across the side yard. I heard the EMTs talking to me as I felt someone pull me away from David. Someone held me up so I wouldn't collapse, as the voices of the EMTs sounded distantly in my brain.

"Can you find a pulse?"

"No."

"Mrs. Hill…Mrs. Hill, can you hear me? How long has he been like this?"

"I don't know," I managed to mumble.

They laid David on the gurney, searching for some sign of life, while positioning an AMBU bag over his nose and mouth, and they began manually pumping oxygen into his lifeless body. An EMT asked, "Does Mr. Hill have a DNR?"

"Yes, we both do."

They took the AMBU bag off.

My best friend, my husband, father of my children, my confidant, my dance partner and the one person who knew me better than anyone on this earth had left me.

The next few weeks were a blur. Claire, Ethan, Carole, Lauren, Katie: the whole family came to be with me. Thankfully, I just handed them David's wishes, and they organized his celebration of life. He never wanted a funeral. And once it was all done and everyone had left, I was alone, completely alone.

All the progress that I had made over the past months went to shit. I wallowed in self-pity, anger, and sorrow for days that turned into months and then turned into years. My beautiful garden, which I had loved so much, was chock full of weeds. My gracious southern home, which I had loved so much, now had paint flaking off the shutters and windows covered in grime. I served on no committees; I communicated with no one. I didn't care.

And now you know why the story begins as it does. That loaded weapon. The old woman at odds with her life and memories; the woman who drinks too much wine and has no idea how her story will end, until maybe she just ends it herself.

I can't write anymore. Since I started putting my story to paper (or, more accurately, in a Word document), I haven't kept track of how long it's been since I began.

But I know it's been many months. Many days it seems like forever. When I think about it, I know I've been writing and narrating my story in my head for almost two decades. There is no ending to write tonight, because I have no ending, other than to make something up. So for now, my story is over. I save my journal and shut my computer down.

I think I'll have some wine. In the kitchen, I grab a glass and a bottle and head to the bedroom, thinking this cannot be how my story ends. I can't continue to be that old woman who sits alone in a rundown house, drinking and mumbling to herself! Something has got to change. I really hope there's some good karma heading my way.

Chapter 32

My eyelids fluttered open the next morning from a very unsettled night of sleep. Yet, oddly, I felt rested. My conscious brain kept trying to pick up bits and pieces of my dreams from the night before. And each dream fragment pulled at me, as if to say, "Don't forget me."

"What the hell does that mean?" I thought.

I tossed the bed sheets aside and thought, "Another day…another damn day alone," but once more I sensed there was something different about today. The sun seemed brighter, and the blue of the sky was crisp and clean, beckoning me to remember something. "What is it?" I wondered.

Sitting up to shuffle into my slippers, I put on my glasses, and I glanced at the nearly empty bottle of merlot from last night and noticed that the top drawer of my nightstand was slightly ajar. Feeling a strong sense of déjà vu, I pulled the drawer fully open. I wondered if I had reloaded the clip in the .22 again last night. But no, the weapon was in its case, and the clip was empty. "Well, that's a sign of progress," I told myself, and thought a good cup of coffee would be great this morning. Maybe the caffeine would help my brain focus on what I needed to remember.

I just couldn't let go of the feeling that I had forgotten something, something that was very important.

I pulled on my old sweater and plodded down the hallway, passing the stack of unopened mail, noticing that the morning's sun was dancing through the front door's glass panes directly on the ever-growing pile of mail.

Something in my mind was still trying desperately to crawl to the surface. But try as I might, I couldn't connect with it. "So strange," I thought to myself and ambled to the kitchen to make some coffee.

As the coffee was brewing, I glimpsed the reflection of myself in the window above the kitchen sink. "When did I get so angry looking?" I wondered. "My reflection is not what it used to be."

"Mattie left a long time ago," I said out loud to the reflection.

The coffee finished brewing, so I filled my cup and wandered back into the hallway. The sun was still gallantly flickering through the dirty windows of my front door, causing me to glance down at the pile of mail.

Sitting near the bottom of the mail, with a brilliant ray of sun hitting the corner of the envelope, it was an overnight letter that had arrived months ago. "Wow seems like a lifetime ago," I thought to myself as I pulled the letter from the pile. I didn't recognize the address but opened it anyway. Taking a welcoming sip of my coffee, I began to read.

Dear Mrs. Hill,

My name is Jeremy, and I am reaching out to you because I have just found out that I am your biological grandson…

I got no further reading the letter as my coffee cup slipped from my hand and crashed to the floor, smashing into pieces. I felt myself desperately holding on to this letter of light as I crumpled to the ground on the foyer floor amid my spilled morning coffee. All I remembered was the glorious light shining through the front windows, casting a glow around me as I lay there thinking, "My baby is back. He found me."

Still clutching the letter, I got myself up amid all the mess on the floor. I didn't care about cleaning up anything; I just walked to the nearest chair, sat down, and continued to read:

Dear Mrs. Hill,

My name is Jeremy, and I am reaching out to you because I have just found out that I am your biological grandson.

I am writing to you because I recently took a 23and-Me DNA test. When I received my results, I was absolutely stunned. Since you also took a DNA test through the same service at some time, my results showed that I shared DNA with a woman called Mattie T. Hill. The results said that the probability of Mattie T. Hill being my biological grandmother was 100%.

When I approached my mom with the results, she was not happy about discussing anything to do with my other family. But she went on to tell me her version of 'the story of me.'

Mom told me that my biological dad is your son; so obviously, you are my biological grandmother; "So Hello!"

Mom was uncomfortable with my questions and her answers were evasive. She didn't give me the answers I craved, so now, I would like to graciously ask you to tell me your version of the 'story of me.'

There are so many questions I want to ask you. And I really want to meet you and my father and learn about my other family. I am hoping that by doing so, I will understand more about the person I am, and the person I strive to be.

Often through my growing up years, I wondered why I felt so different because I was nothing like my brothers. There is a fire in me that just never seems to be quenched. I have little in common with my siblings, and that bothers me, plus I don't look anything like them. Mom just put it off as different genes playing their part in our family dynamics.

Please don't misunderstand me. I have a wonderful life with my parents, and I know they love me. There is just something always there, right on the edge that I feel, but can't quite grasp. It's a feeling that makes me think that I just don't quite belong; that I am just an honorary member of the family.

When I was young and did something free or unexpected or tell Mom and Dad about my desires to go hunting and fishing, or ride horses, or maybe go in the military (I loved to play soldiers, and I loved playing with my cars when I was a kid), my parents would always give a look to each other, and it made me curious, even as a young child. Kids pick up on those unspoken things between their parents.

So, upon graduating from high school I decided to go against my parents' wishes and applied for entrance into the Citadel (they wanted me to go to Clemson or Alabama). Amazingly enough, I was accepted at the Citadel. I have truly excelled in the military environment, and I love it.

Anyway, with that being said, I am now 22 years old, which I know you are aware of, and about to graduate from the Citadel Military College, and plan to continue in a military career after graduation.

I hope to hear from you sooner than later so that we can talk. You will find my contact info included in the package.

Also, I have not told my parents this, but please find enclosed an invitation for you and my biological father (Mom did tell me his name is Ethan) to attend my graduation. I hope it is not too hard of a journey for either of you. It is very important to me that you are both present at my graduation.

I'm looking forward to hearing from you and I hope to see you and Ethan soon. Please call me, so you can let me know if either or both of you can make it to my graduation.

Your Grandson,
Jeremy Dawson

As I read that letter over and over again, I suddenly realized there was more in the package. I dug into the envelope and pulled out two invitations, one for me and one for Ethan, and Jeremy's contact information. As I read the date on the invitation, I realized it was only two weeks away! Scrambling to find my phone, I called Ethan. When he answered, I read your letter to him.

We both cried uncontrollably. The child we had lost had found us.

We had to make arrangements and quickly, so Ethan took charge of travel arrangements, and I called my grandson.

My hands shook as I dialed his number. It went to voicemail so, hoping I didn't sound too nervous from excitement, I left my grandson a message. "Jeremy, this is Mattie, your grandmother. I am so sorry it has taken me so long to respond to you. Ethan and I will be honored to witness your graduation. Hopefully we'll see you soon. Please call me when you get the chance. My heart is so full of joy that you have reached out and found me. I can't wait to hear from you."

As soon as I had finished the voice mail, my phone rang. I didn't know the number, and as always, I was hesitant to answer unknown calls. But this time I did. And boy was I glad.

I answered the call with a soft "Hello."

"Nana, this is Jeremy."

Everything in my being tried to remain calm and behave normally, but it wasn't to be. I couldn't reply because I couldn't control the overwhelming emotion of happiness that enveloped me just hearing his voice and hearing him call me Nana.

"Nana, are you there?"

After a few more seconds, I replied, "Yes, Jeremy, I'm here. I'm sorry that I didn't respond immediately, but I am so excited to hear your voice after all these years; it just took my breath away. I can't believe I'm actually on the phone with you. God, I've missed you. Please tell me everything about you. I want to hear everything."

The hours flew by as Jeremy talked about his growing up years, only slightly hinting about his unsettled feeling of not fitting in with his family. I just listened and relished hearing his deep voice that was punctuated with a soft southern drawl. Suddenly, there was a slight silence. Hesitantly, he asked, "Nana, please tell me what happened between your family and my mom."

"Oh, Jeremy, that story is a very long one, and if you are okay with it, I would rather wait until Ethan is with us so we can all talk about it together," I replied.

"I need to know something now, Nana," he declared.

"Okay, I will tell you this, Jeremy. Your grandfather and I were going to adopt you upon your birth. That's how much we wanted you in our lives."

I heard him gasp on the phone. "What? What are you talking about? I never was told that," he exclaimed.

"Jeremy, as I said, our story, your story, is one of many twists and turns. I have actually written a journal about it over the last several months. Would you like me to send it to you?"

"Absolutely, Nana," he replied.

"Remember, Jeremy, the words that are written tell my story and my story only. Sometimes I am harsh with my words about your mom's family, only because that is what I felt at the time. Please do not hold any of it against me or your mom. It's a story about life, and unfortunately life can be ugly at times."

"I understand. I'll do my best to remain unbiased when I read it."

"All right, then. I'll send you a PDF of it when we hang up. Remember to keep an open mind. I know it was a very difficult journey for both our families. And I truly believe that your mom made decisions that she thought were in your very best interest. And obviously everything worked out okay."

Again, there was a moment of silence before Jeremy replied. "Yes, I'm okay, but I'm not whole."

It was my turn to be quiet. It took me a moment to gather my thoughts before I responded.

"Jeremy, no family is whole when they have been separated, whether by distance or a falling out or by other circumstances. When that happens, you always feel like a piece of the puzzle that makes up *you* is missing," I answered.

"That's exactly right, Nana, and you are that piece of the puzzle. I am so glad I found you. I already feel connected to you."

I simply stated the obvious. "You've always been right here with me, Jeremy. When you were born, the first words I whispered to you were, 'No matter where you are, or who you are with, you are my soul. and now that you're here, I will never lose you. You are a part of me.'"

I heard Jeremy sniffling on the other end of the phone. "Jeremy, please don't cry. There have been enough tears during this journey. Let's focus on all the happy memories we now get to make. I'll talk to you soon. Sleep well, my boy. I love you."

"Good night, Nana. I love you too."

Chapter 33

I sent Jeremy my story after we ended our call. I prayed fervently that he would not be angry with me or his mother. Or, heaven forbid, he would read it and then not want Ethan or me to go to his graduation! I couldn't dwell on any of that, because I was going to see him in a week!

I also texted Ethan that I had talked to Jeremy.

He called me immediately.

"Oh my God, Mom. How did he sound? Why didn't you call me? Is he excited about seeing us? Where and when are we going to meet him?"

"He sounded great, and yes, he is excited about seeing us. I don't have the details yet on when and where, but, Ethan, he wanted to know why we were not involved in his life. He only knows his mom's side of the story. I decided to send him my story."

Ethan was furious. "You did what! Mom, you sent your journal, or "story" as you call it, to me and Claire months ago and told us to "keep it just between us," which is what I did. And I know Claire did. Now you're sending it to Jeremy? He's going to be so mad when he reads it. Hell, I was mad when I read it! What if he doesn't want us to come after he finishes reading it?"

"Son, everything will be okay. He will know that none of us ever stopped loving him or missing him. We must have faith, just one more time."

"I am so tired of you saying that. After all these years of you saying, 'Have faith, everything will be okay,' it hasn't been okay, and I'm over it! I'm telling you Mom, if sending that story to him jeopardizes us meeting him, I don't know if I'll be able to forgive you."

Sharply, I replied, "Ethan, if sending my story to Jeremy compromises our upcoming visit with him, I won't be able to forgive myself! I'll keep you updated," and hung up.

I made appointments for my hair, a facial and waxing, a pedicure and manicure in preparation for Jeremy's graduation: everything that I had neglected for years, while dwelling on whether I had made the right decision by sending him my story. Ethan was right. What had I done? Why couldn't I have left it alone? But Jeremy wanted to know his story. Please Lord, please don't let me have made the wrong decision.

I decided I would go shopping and splurged on some fun, colorful dresses that were flattering for mature women and spring sandals that were stylish yet sensible. I sure didn't want to trip or fall because of shoes that I couldn't walk in comfortably.

I wanted Jeremy to be proud of me.

While I was shopping, Ethan called and told me that he had arranged his flight and booked us in a bed-and-breakfast near the campus.

"Are you still angry with me? I asked.

"Yeah, I am. Until you hear back from him, I will remain mad," Ethan replied.

"I'm sorry. I thought it would be a good thing to do. I may have been wrong."

"Mom, just let me know when he contacts you, okay?"

"I will, son."

A day passed, and then two. Jeremy had not called. I debated about calling him but refrained because I didn't want to be that hovering grandmother. I had already screwed up in the eyes of my son. But damn, it was worrying me something fierce. I decided I needed to go for a walk to clear my mind and have a moment to quietly talk to God. About halfway through my walk, my phone rang. It was Jeremy.

"Hello, Jeremy."

"Hey, Nana," he said quietly. "I read your story. It made me very sad and really furious. I'm having a hard time dealing with what I read."

"Oh crap, I've screwed everything up," I thought.

Quickly composing myself, I said, "It is a tough narrative to read, Jeremy. But I hope that you realize that I never meant to hurt anyone by writing it. It was a way to help myself heal."

"Yeah, I guess I know that. But I am hurt. I am hurt that I didn't know any of this. I'm sad that you were so angry for so long. And I am furious that I was denied knowing my other family, who obviously loved me and who wanted me desperately in their lives."

"Are you going to talk to your mom about what you have learned?" I asked.

"Yes, I will. But not now. What's most important to me is seeing you and Ethan. By the way, may I have my father's cell phone number? I'd like to call him."

Finally, all my decade-long conversations with God had finally been answered. I gave Jeremy Ethan's number, and as I said goodbye, I simultaneously texted Ethan that Jeremy would be calling him and added that everything was okay.

What a conversation that would be!

Ethan called me several hours later. "Did you talk to Jeremy?" I asked.

"I did, and, Mom, it was the hardest phone call and the best phone call all rolled into one. He was angry with me, and rightfully so. I acknowledged his anger, and then it seemed that we were both so grateful to be speaking with one another that our conversation went smoothly from then on. Mom, he really wants us in his life. Although he did say he needed to ask me some serious questions."

"Well, that's to be expected, son. He probably needs to know why you weren't in his life to begin with. And you'll just have to be honest with him."

"I know that, Mom, but I'm scared. If he does ask me and I'm honest and tell him what a screwup I was when he was born, will he still want to see me?'

"Ethan, I think he will respect your honesty. Just tell him the truth. I think Jeremy is a young man searching to find out who he is and where he came from. Let's not fret about it now, because in a few short days we will actually be able to see him, hug him, and talk to him face-to-face after all these years. And it will be a glorious day."

I continued by saying, "I've done something a bit crazy, son."

"Mom, what the hell? What have you done now?"

"Do you remember the stocking that Sara made for Jeremy all those years ago?"

"Yes."

"Well, I've pulled it out of the attic, and I've filled it up with lots of candy, protein bars, a lottery card, and a Starbucks card. I plan on giving it to him when we see him."

"Mom, you can't hand him a stocking at his graduation."

"Watch me."

We ended our conversation, both eagerly waiting for our trip to the Citadel.

Chapter 34

The day began as so many of them do in the historic city of Charleston. At least that's the way I imagined how each day would start, though it was only my third visit to the Holy City. The birds were softly chattering the early news of the day, the nocturnal animals were beginning their descent to slumber at dawn's early light, and the first hint of the coastal spring warmth was beginning to welcome all with open arms.

The day before, I had driven the hour-and-half journey from Beaufort and arrived in town safe yet exhausted. I, frankly, was quite proud of myself for this accomplishment, being a seventy-two-year-old woman a bit past her prime for such a journey on her own. No wrong turns, no flat tires, and no issues with anyone trying to put one over on an unsuspecting lady of the gray-haired persuasion. Lucky me!

Ethan had flown in earlier, and he had checked us in at the local bed-and-breakfast that he had reserved. I met him for a light supper at a local café, and after supper I told Ethan that I needed to get a good night's sleep before tomorrow's graduation. That was my hope, anyway. But unfortunately, my mind would not rest. So around 4:00 a.m. I gave up, got dressed, and headed outside to explore. But there was no need to worry. I had my trusty .22 with me!

My roaming proved worthwhile as I found a wonderful public garden that was open 24-7. The beautiful refuge was traversed with wandering paths paralleled by stately live oaks, river birch, and other coastal greenery. It was here that I pondered the last twenty plus years, wondering whether those questions asked and unanswered in all the years prior would somehow be answered today. It was also along this path that I questioned the choices that I had made and how they may affect today's outcome. Some of my mind's meanderings brought memories of such grave sadness that I found myself wiping away stray tears among the mix of the fine sheen of dampness that caressed my face in the early morning sultriness.

I continued my stroll through the wonderful gardens, pausing here and there to marvel at the beauty of the spring fauna. Up ahead I noticed an area of the path where a weathered wooden park bench was perfectly nestled among the dripping wisteria, confederate jasmine, and Spanish moss, creating a soft, aromatic early-dawn-filtered canopy. The bench was covered with carvings: "Lindsey loves Sam," "Class of '15," and numerous other notes of memories that were carefully remembered here. "I'm sure this bench has some stories to tell," I thought.

Having not slept much the night before, the old body was telling me that I was not as young as my ego wished I was. Thinking I should have stopped for some morning caffeine, I settled on the bench for a short rest and, of course, continued pondering about all the years that had passed yet excitedly looking forward to the future.

I drifted off to sleep.

I was suddenly aware of the sun's rays dancing brightly upon my face, not to mention my old bones grumbling about sitting so long on a very uncomfortable wooden bench.

Damn, I am old. I fell asleep in a dang park! As I struggled to wake up, my cell phone rang. It was Ethan.

"Mom, where are you? It's 7:30 a.m. We were supposed to meet for breakfast at 7:00 a.m.!"

"Sorry, son. I went for a walk and fell asleep in a park," I replied.

"Mom, you can't be serious. You fell asleep in a park? Do you know how dangerous that is?"

"Don't yell at me, Ethan. Yes, I know that was stupid, but I just fell asleep. I'm fine, and I'm heading back now. I'll be there in a few minutes," I said.

Ethan continued to chastise me for being so reckless, so I simply hung up, grabbed a cup of coffee from Starbucks and walked the few blocks back to the B&B. Before entering, I texted Jeremy to let him know again how thrilled we were to be a part of his celebration.

Immediately, my phone chimed. "Nana, I can't wait to see you and Ethan. Remember, Commencement starts promptly at 9:00 a.m. Please try to arrive early to get a good seat. By the way, I still haven't told my parents. I'll deal with them later. I'll meet you after commencement in Tilghman Courtyard. Wait for me."

I brushed happy tears from my face as I entered the B&B. Ethan was waiting in the foyer, ready to resume reciting the riot act to me for my irresponsible behavior.

I quickly gave him a mom look, showed him Jeremy's text, and said, "I'll be down in thirty minutes."

Showered, makeup applied, and hair done, I put on one of my new dresses with some low-heeled canvas sandals. "I'm glad I got that pedicure and the facial wax," I thought. As many proper southern ladies know, "If you don't have a good pedicure, you are not properly attired. And, if you have those errant chin whiskers, you need to go home and hide!"

I completed my outfit by putting on Mamaw's diamond necklace that Poppa had given me all those years ago and the diamond earrings that David had given me when we were newlyweds. I put on my diamond wedding band and my special ring from David (it was a huge four carat Peridot) and looked at the finished product in the mirror.

"Okay, not bad for a grandmother. You look understated yet classy," I said out loud to the reflection in the mirror. Gazing a few seconds more at the image before me, I was amazed at how it now appeared. Yes, it was still wrinkled and gray haired, yet, thankfully, the look of anger and despair was gone. Now, my sky-blue eyes shone brightly: filled with life and love and hope for the future.

"Thank God I opened Jeremy's letter. It saved my life. Someone was definitely looking after me." Chuckling, I thought, "Maybe it was the lady in the clouds."

Grabbing my purse and Jeremy's Christmas stocking, I headed downstairs to meet Ethan.

Our Uber was waiting outside the B&B to take us to campus. It was 8:15 a.m., and traffic was horrendous heading to the Corps of Cadets commencement. Although it was just May, spring had bypassed South Carolina completely. It was a full-fledged summer day: a sultry eighty-nine degrees already, not counting the humidity. As we crawled along in the Uber, I knew my beautifully coiffed and straight-ironed hair was beginning to spring into its unruly curls. "It is what it is," I thought as I wiped beads of perspiration off my neck. My excessive moisture was probably not only due to the heat but also compounded by my nerves and the anticipation of seeing my Jeremy. Finally.

We arrived on campus and entered the McAlister Field House with invitations in hand. We found two seats together near the middle, and Ethan, never letting go of my hand, courteously excused us as we made our way passed other proud family members and friends that were already seated in the row. Taking our seats,

Ethan and I fidgeted with excitement. Somewhere in the crowd of almost a thousand graduates, family members, and friends of graduates was my grandson, Jeremy. We had found him after seventeen years. Actually, he had found us.

We sat together, vaguely hearing the speeches and accolades of the numerous speakers and their accomplishments—and we were completely bored. We were very thankful when the President of the Citadel, a retired Marine, moved to the podium and addressed the graduates and families.

"Soon we'll see Jeremy cross the stage," I whispered to Ethan. He grabbed my hand tightly and, with tears of happiness in his eyes, said, "I know, Mom. I can't believe we're here; we've waited so long to see him again. Are you nervous?"

"Damn straight I am. Are you?'

"Mom, I have never been this nervous in all my life. I cannot wait to see my son."

It seemed to take forever for the colonel to begin announcing the graduates whose last names began with *D*. And then, like magic, we heard "Jeremy Crawford Dawson."

Ethan and I both stood up to catch a glimpse of Jeremy after all these years. Even from such a distance, I instantly recognized the young boy that now was a striking young man. Resplendent in his cadet uniform, he strode across the stage to accept his diploma. As he looked out into the crowd that was politely applauding a young man's accomplishment, Ethan and I couldn't help ourselves. We waved frantically and locked eyes on the young man a hundred yards away from us, praying that he would somehow see us. As he gazed out over the crowded stadium, he tilted his head ever so slightly in recognition. We both fell to our seats, complete in knowing that Jeremy had seen us. Oh, how my heart danced with happiness. Thank you, Lord. We've been waiting for this for so friggin' long.

Ethan and I were impatient, waiting for the pomp and circumstance to end.

Two hours later, it was finally over. We immediately rose from our seats and gathered with the throngs of other family members and friends attempting to exit the field house. Finally, we emerged into the midday heat of Charleston, and my phone chimed. It was Jeremy. I looked at Ethan in apprehension. "Oh, please don't let there be an issue," I said to him.

"Mom, have faith. He reached out to us. It's obvious Jeremy wants to be in our lives again."

Hugging my son fiercely, I said, "Wow, now you're telling me to have faith! But that's exactly what your dad would have told me."

I read Jeremy's text out loud. It simply said, "I'll meet you in the courtyard in thirty minutes."

We navigated our way to Tilghman Courtyard, named in honor of Horace L. "Son" Tilghman and his wife, Kitty Lou Tilghman. According to the information I read about the location, it is a favorite spot for Citadel visitors to gather. And today was no exception. The courtyard was crowded. It was not the secluded spot I had envisioned for our reunion. But did that really matter? No, not one bit!

It was now 12:20 p.m. "Just a few more minutes," I thought. My stomach twisted over and over as my heart thumped loudly in my ears from excitement and nerves.

Looking down at my watch, it read 12:35 p.m. "Oh, dear God, please don't let this journey go unanswered," I thought. Ethan tugged on my arm and, glancing at the family walking down the path to the courtyard, I instantly knew it wasn't Jeremy and told Ethan so.

"Mom, look at the people behind that family," he directed.

Gazing farther down the sidewalk, I saw a young man: tall and slender yet muscular in his build, with strawberry blond hair. It was him! My heart just about exploded right then and there. My eyes began to tear at the intense joy of just seeing him: my child, my grandson...the one I've thought about for so long. The child I had lost and had now found again. "Hold yourself together, old girl, right now," I demanded of myself as I clutched Ethan's arm for support. I truly think Ethan and I were holding each other up at that moment.

He looked so handsome, dressed in his crisp uniform adorned with medals that acknowledged his accomplishments during his schooling at the Citadel. His hair was closely cropped, military style, with a slight curl along his forehead, just like Ethan's. His eyes, even from this distance, were still the crisp sky blue that I remembered, just like mine and just like his father's.

Oh, damn, he's with his family! Of course he's with his family. How could I even think that they wouldn't be with him?

I literally felt like I was going to be sick. There is no freaking way I want to be reunited with Jeremy while they were nearby. It wouldn't be right. This is supposed to be our time, dammit.

Then, as I watched, he turned to his mother, grabbed her hand, and spoke gently in her ear. He pointed in our direction. His family stopped walking and looked our way. I swear it appeared as if Jeremy's family began to swarm around Megan, as if protecting the queen bee. But she locked eyes with me and, never wavering, nodded in my direction. She let go of Jeremy's hand, as if releasing my long-lost child back to me.

His other grandparents of course did not accept this, and Ethan and I watched as they heatedly conversed with Megan and Jeremy. Ethan and I stood, holding hands, waiting and watching.

Their conversation continued for a few moments longer, and then abruptly Jeremy threw up his hands, kissed his mother on the cheek, and said as clear as day, "You can continue this worthless dialogue without me. I have made my decision, and my decision is to spend time with my other family." At that moment, I felt the earth shift ever so slightly, as if the good Lord had finally decided that today was the day that He would answer my prayers. He was now righting my world, and my family's world.

And Jeremy had just rocked *their* perfect world.

Chapter 35

My grandson walked away from the only family that he had known for over seventeen years. He walked purposefully and proudly, directly toward us. As he drew closer, none of us could stand still any longer. We ran straight into each other's arms! And, in that instant, as we wept and hugged each other, my world was finally right.

My boy was back in my arms again.

After a few moments, we composed ourselves, and Jeremy held out his hand to me and said to us, "Let's go for a walk. It's now time for us. We have a lot of catching up to do." I held on to that boy's hand like my life depended on it. And it did.

I looked up at my grandson's face and said, "Jeremy, this isn't right. This is what happened to me and to my family. We must do the right thing. We cannot just walk away from your family."

Ethan looked at me in astonishment. "Mom, what are you talking about? You have had years of misery because of decisions made by this family."

"Yes, that's true, but it is time someone steps up and tries to mend all these wounds." Ethan looked at his son, and Jeremy said, "She's right, Ethan, and we both know it."

Ethan, Jeremy, and I walked hand in hand toward Megan and her family. We were about thirty yards away, and we still could hear their heated conversation. Jeremy's grandmother purposely turned her back to us. I truly hoped Jeremy had not seen that!

Megan saw us approaching. She pulled away from her family, hesitating for just a brief moment, and then began walking toward us. As the distance between us shortened with each of our footsteps, I hoped this walk would be one of healing and forgiveness for us all.

Jeremy's family finally stopped their conversation and looked in bewilderment at the scene unfolding before them. Megan wasn't walking anymore; she was running toward us. "Oh, crap, is she going to take Jeremy from us again?" I thought frantically.

She didn't. She simply ran right up to Ethan and grabbed his shoulders. Looking directly into his eyes, she said, "I'm so sorry, Ethan, for the pain I have caused your family, and especially you and your mom. Please forgive me. I should have spoken up years ago, because I knew it was the wrong decision. I just wasn't strong enough." I was completely stunned by Megan's apology, because I had wanted to hear those words for years.

The four of us stood awkwardly in a wide circle, waiting for Ethan to respond to her apology. The seconds slowly ticked by until, finally, Ethan reacted. "Oh, Lord," I thought, "please don't be an ass, son."

He wasn't. He tenderly gathered her in his arms, and said, "Megan, I'm sorry as well. You are not the only one who was not strong enough. I failed you, and I completely failed Jeremy as a father. You have been an amazing mom, and I thank you for being there for our son. Look at all you have accomplished. He is an amazing young man." As Jeremy's parents held each other, I watched silently as my grandson walked over and enveloped them both in forgiveness.

That moment is forever etched in my mind and my heart. That was the moment that healing finally began for my family. For both our families. And it was in that moment that I realized that not only had I lost Jeremy all those years ago; I had also lost myself. Even though I had tried so hard to reinvent myself without him, I was nothing without Jeremy. Now, watching them hug, laugh, cry, and talk all at the same time, I knew that I had not only found Jeremy again but that I had also found Mattie.

I glanced over at Megan's family, not budging from where Megan had left them. Their faces said it all: disbelief, disgust, and, yup, anger. They still didn't think we were good enough to be part of Jeremy's life.

"Oh, well," I thought to myself. "It's our time now. Jeremy thinks we are good enough. You're just experiencing a taste of the rejection I have lived with for years. Karma can be a bitch!"

I know, that was not a kind thing to think, but it's what I felt. Perhaps in a few years, maybe eighteen or so, I'll be able to forgive Megan's family. But just maybe.

As Megan pulled away from her son and Ethan, she looked my way. I was still standing away from the three of them, and I knew from the look in her eyes she needed me to make the first move.

My mind immediately went into protective mode. "Should I? After all the years of sorrow and emptiness, can I take that first step? Sure I *can*. But will I?"

Looking down at my clenched fists, I just couldn't do it.

Chapter 36

I just couldn't let another human being experience what I had lived through. I began walking toward her, and in seconds we were in each other's arms. Not saying a word to each other, we just stood in the courtyard holding on to one another, and as we did, the years of pain ebbed away, and the light of forgiveness filled my heart. Finally, I found my voice and whispered, "Thank you for giving me back my grandchild. I am so grateful."

Our sons walked over and joined us. As Megan and I released each other from our embrace, we wiped each other's tears away and just looked at each other, woman to woman, mother to mother. No more words were necessary. Megan had always known that I would never have abandoned or forgotten Jeremy. And she now knew that I forgave her: not her family, but her.

Jeremy, breaking that silent moment of reconciliation, said, "Mom, again, I'm sorry to ruin the plans for this afternoon. I love you all so much, but I want to spend this afternoon with Ethan and Nana. It is what I want to do. Give me a moment so I can go tell everyone what I'm going to do."

And, by God, that's exactly what he did. He strode over to them, and we watched in disbelief as he told them that he was going with us, his other family. As I watched him walk away from them, I knew exactly what they were feeling, watching their loved one leave.

We said goodbye to Megan, and then Ethan, Jeremy, and I walked arm in arm out of the campus, hailed a taxi and spent the rest of the day exploring the beautiful town of Charleston, South Carolina.

We strolled through the graceful city streets, lined with ancient trees draped in years of Spanish moss, and nodded to the other happy Citadel graduates and their families as we passed. My son and I were with Jeremy, our son and grandson, and we were a family.

Our conversations were easy and free flowing, as if we had never been apart all those years. We talked on and on about Jeremy's plans for the future, about what he wanted to see and experience. Ethan and I never took our eyes off him as he spoke about his goals. We were mesmerized by his confidence as he spoke about his plans and how he would achieve those goals. As he continued to speak about his hopes for his military career, I witnessed the same enthusiasm that Ethan had demonstrated when he was in the Corps. Like father, like son: they had the same gift of speaking with charisma and confidence. And they both loved the military.

I was a happy old girl, and the light that had once been snuffed out so coldly decades ago was now burning brightly. Everyone has experienced that light—and the loss of it. It is the light that keeps you going, the one that enables you to take that next step and then the next. Even when everything in your being says it's fruitless, you continue, because you know that if you don't hold on to the light, however dim it may have become, you will lose your identity.

"Memorize these precious moments," I demanded of myself quietly. "I'm not sure how many more of these we will get to share, so don't ever forget this special time. He has always been a part of you, and you a part of him."

The very same words I had whispered to him when he was born.

Chapter 37

Eventually we stopped at the same Starbucks that I had visited earlier that morning. For some reason it had a different atmosphere that afternoon. It just wasn't a coffee shop; now it had become a place for new memories. We were here with Jeremy! Could I not be more content? I wish I could have pinched myself without being obvious, to make sure that this was real. (Okay, I did pinch myself, but very discreetly, of course.)

After placing our orders, we grabbed the first available table. I asked Jeremy if he had any questions for us. There was just a slight hesitation, and then he quietly asked, "Nana, I've read your story, and Ethan and I have talked. But I have so many questions that I just don't know where to begin."

"Well, let's start with the question that you want answered the most," I replied. This time Jeremy didn't hesitate, although he did shift uncomfortably in his seat as he leaned toward Ethan. "I've heard my mother's story. Now I want you to tell me in your own words why you left me. We didn't really talk about that when we spoke on the phone. I wanted to be face-to-face with you when I asked you this question and to hear your answer."

The silence around our table was thick with emotion. Ethan touched his son's shoulder and said, "Give me a moment, Jeremy. I need to go outside and gather my thoughts before I tell you my side of the story."

I watched Ethan quickly leave the coffee shop and walk down the sidewalk out of sight.

As difficult as it was, Jeremy and I continued to make idle conversation as we waited for Ethan to return. After about ten minutes, Ethan walked back in, controlled and ready to tell his story.

As he sat down at the table, he looked directly at his son and said, "Jeremy, I screwed up royally. I was a scared, immature, and irresponsible young adult. I partied too much and was not doing well in school. I had no way to support you. And honestly, your mom didn't want to have anything to do with me. I had no future until my parents read me the riot act and told me to join the Corps. None of these reasons excuse my actions. Every day prior to today was a day of regret, because I had not been there for you as a father should.

"Please know that I have never, ever stopped loving you and wishing that I had made different decisions. If you can find it in your heart, I ask your forgiveness. I am a different person now. And I would be so grateful, and honored, if you would allow me to be a part of your life, in whatever manner you would be comfortable with."

As I listened to my son explain his faults, which I was completely aware of, I watched Jeremy's expression. It said nothing. And he said nothing as he continued to look into his father's eyes. I swear my heart stopped beating as we both waited for a response. The seconds ticked by in silence, when suddenly Jeremy pushed his chair back, got up from the table, and left. I jumped from my seat to follow him. Ethan grabbed my arm. "Mom, let him be," he said. "He will either leave or come back."

"But that's not a freaking option, Ethan! You don't understand. I cannot lose him again," I exclaimed.

"Mom, we've been blessed with today. I truly believe he'll be back. He just has to digest what I just told him."

"Screw that, Ethan. I'm going to go find him!"

And then my son said to me, "Mom, just have faith in Jeremy."

Suddenly, my grandson's voice whispered behind me: "Nana, you don't need to find me anymore. I'm right here. We are no longer lost to each other, because we have found each other. Remember, I read your story, and I now know with my whole heart that you, my father, and my other family tried everything they could to keep me in their lives."

I turned around, and as Jeremy extended his arms to hug me, I fell into them, so grateful that my grandson now knew everything.

We left Starbucks and continued walking through Charleston. Our stories and conversations lasted the rest of the day and into the early evening. Jeremy questions revolved around how we grew up, what we liked to do, what we liked to eat. Whether we were Republicans or Democrats. One of his questions that really stood out to me was whether we believed in God. Ethan looked at me with that look saying, "You answer first."

"Yes, I still believe in God. Yet I have been mad at Him for years. I lost my faith years ago because all my prayers about keeping you in our lives obviously went unanswered. But God has a funny way of answering prayers in His own time, doesn't He?"

"So, you lost your faith when you could no longer see me. Is that right, Nana?"

"I'm sad to say this, Jeremy, but that sums it up pretty well," I replied.

"I appreciate your honesty, Nana. So, Ethan, what are your thoughts on God?"

Ethan did not respond for several minutes as we continued to walk.

And then my son said, "I was raised as a Catholic, and I was brought up to believe in right and wrong and forgiveness of others and ourselves. But I lost my faith a long time ago because I have never been able to forgive myself."

"Forgive yourself for what?" Jeremy asked.

"I never should have signed those adoption papers. I never realized that putting my signature on those documents would mean that none of our family would have any contact with you from that time onward. And neither did my mom. She was assured that we would still be able to visit with you."

"Is that really your fault?" Jeremy asked. "I know you were told one thing, and I also now know that the reason they wanted the papers signed was that it would make their lives easier. They wouldn't have to explain to anyone why I didn't look like my siblings. I have forgiven my parents for their concealment over the years. Isn't it about time to forgive yourself? You are my father by blood, and today, from this minute forward, we have an opportunity to create a bond as father and son. Don't you agree?"

Jeremy had just called my son his father!

Ethan stopped walking and hugged his Jeremy fiercely. "Dammit, son, I have missed you for so long. My world has never been right since we lost you, and I so want to be there for you from now on."

As they released each other, Jeremy said to us, "I was really scared about us meeting. I really didn't know what to expect, but I kind of did. I knew from our phone conversations that you guys understood me. I was so comfortable talking with you both. It felt like home. And now I am completely assured that my newfound family never wanted to lose me. I wish we could get all those years back."

"Oh, Jeremy, we do as well. But we've got lots of years ahead of us to make some great memories," Ethan said.

We hugged again on the sidewalk, a family reunited.

The sun had already started its daily descent; the shadows were playing their beautiful dance among the leaves of the old trees along the streets of this lovely city. I suggested we go for a final walk to the garden I'd discovered that morning. I couldn't believe it had been just a few hours ago that I'd ventured along those garden paths, with the beautiful dawn sunlight dancing through the trees. It surely is amazing how a few hours can change your life.

I guided my boys to the same bench that I had fallen asleep on earlier that morning. As we sat together in the balmy evening dusk, it became apparent that our day together was drawing to a close.

I looked at the beautiful young man that had filled my life for such a few short years yet was always a part of me. I kissed his cheek and murmured, "Thank you, Jeremy, for sending that letter. You saved my life. But I'm really tired, and I need to go to bed." He held my wrinkled, veined hands in his strong young ones and simply replied, "I know, Nana. We shall never say good-bye again. We will just say, 'See you later.'"

"Sounds like a wonderful plan to me," I replied.

Jeremy stood up, still resplendent in his uniform, and turned to his father. Ethan stood up, erect, prepared to address an officer, and saluted his son. Jeremy saluted back, and then they were in each other's arms.

We shared numerous hugs as we said prolonged goodbyes, Not one of us wanted to leave each other, but we all knew our first reunion was over. Jeremy had to go back to his other family.

Ethan and I watched as Jeremy walked away. To be honest, Ethan literally had to hold me up as I watched my grandchild walk away. It had been a beautiful day, but I had let him go so many times before. Why would this time be any different? Yes it would be, you silly old woman: your grandson found *you*.

We walked back, mother and son, to the B&B, happy with the fact that Jeremy would now be a part of our family. "We have to call Claire and tell her," I said to Ethan.

"I'll do it, Mom; you're really tired."

He was absolutely correct. I was exhausted yet elated. I went to my room, got in my jammies, and fell instantly asleep. That night I slept undisturbed, not threatened by nasty dreams or unwanted demons. The next morning, I awoke completely refreshed and whole. I was a grand-mother again.

Chapter 38

Since our trip to the Citadel, Ethan and I have been in constant contact with Jeremy. He texts or calls one of us weekly. In addition, we have spent many weekends together over the summer since his graduation. Many times, he and Ethan would meet and drive down to stay with me for a long weekend. There were times that Claire was able to leave the vet practice and join us.

On those mornings when we were all together, Jeremy, Ethan, and Claire would gather around the kitchen island in their pj's, talking for hours about anything and everything while I happily prepared a hearty southern breakfast while listening to their animated chatter. Often, Jeremy would bombard us with questions about his newly found family. Most of his questions centered around Ethan, Claire, and me. "What did we like to do when we were young? What were our favorite memories growing up? How did everyone get into riding horses? What was it like growing up near the water?" He sat entranced, like a wide-eyed little boy, soaking in our answers and our memories as if they were from another world and another time.

Which is exactly what they were.

On one occasion I asked Ethan to grab the old photo albums from the top shelf in my closet. Everyone sat around the kitchen island eagerly as I wiped off the years of accumulated dust from their covers.

Grabbing the first cleaned album, Ethan gasped after he opened it and glanced at the first page of photos. "Is that really you in those skintight tie-dyed hip-huggers, Mom?"

Ethan turned the album to show Jeremy and Claire.

"Oh my God, Mom, you have feather earrings and a halter top. You look like you just attended Woodstock," Claire exclaimed.

"Yup, that's me. And no, Woodstock was before my time. The ole body has changed a wee bit, hasn't it? There's no hip-huggers in my future, that's for sure!"

"Look at Dad," Claire chirped in. "He has an Afro and look at the white bell-bottomed suit he's wearing!"

"Your father was hot stuff back then, and it wasn't an Afro. He just had curly hair," I told them.

"Mom, you have curly hair. That shit that dad had was an Afro," Ethan said.

"Be respectful, Ethan."

"What am I supposed to be respectful of? Dad's hair?"

As we all laughed, Jeremy gathered up the rest of the now cleaned photo albums and said "Why don't we all go into the family room? It'll be more comfortable there."

"Sure, let's do that. Mom, should we put another pot of coffee on?" asked Ethan.

"Actually, I was thinking about making a pitcher of margaritas since we're having tacos for dinner. And it is after 12:00 p.m. somewhere! How does that sound?"

Everyone agreed that was a great idea, so as they began looking through the photos in the family room, I busied myself making the pitcher of Mexican nectar.

I brought the pitcher and glasses into the family room and served everyone a chilled marguerita as we carefully examined every detail of the photos of

Mamaw, Poppa, Aunt Carole, Aunt Lauren, David, and the whole clan. Everyone would laugh a little too heartily when they viewed the photos of David and me in our younger years.

It was a wonderful day.

I felt so complete and so thoroughly happy during those times. And, yes, I felt lucky.

Lucky that I was a part of my family making memories together.

Since our reunion, my heart has healed. I am no longer angry, and I sleep peacefully. I love wandering through my home now. It is always clean, with beautiful light shining through the beveled windows, accenting the photos that I had packed up years ago of Jeremy as a baby and young boy, that now stood proudly displayed among our recently framed photos of Ethan, Jeremy, Claire, and me on numerous outings, sitting together in my back yard, and yes there were shots of those always-silly selfies! But none of them sported those awful fish lips!

Chapter 39

It is now October, and Jeremy is scheduled to leave for his first assignment in two weeks.

A week prior to Jeremy's departure, I invited him and Ethan for lunch. Thankfully, both boys replied that they would be able to make it for my luncheon. Unfortunately, Claire couldn't get the time off.

The day before the luncheon was a spectacular fall day. The Carolina-blue sky was dotted with fluffy white clouds that glided and morphed in a wonderful waltz in the cool fall wind. I spent a lot of that day working in the back garden, listening to the song of the crisp leaves as they tap-danced against each other as I planted chrysanthemums and put out pumpkins in preparation for the fall season. Now that my family is complete, my desire to make my beloved home look pretty and loved has become a top priority for me.

I also prepared a shrimp étouffée for our lunch the following day. (Making it a day early was the ticket to étouffée. It allows the flavors to develop and refine the whole dish.) All I would have to do tomorrow was to warm it up before serving.

As I happily readied myself for bed that evening, I sent Ethan and Jeremy a text. "Lunch will be served tomorrow at 1:00 p.m. We're having Shrimp Etouffee, and since the weather looks great for tomorrow, we'll eat outside in the back garden. I've spent most of the day working out back, and it looks so lovely. If I'm not in the house, I'll be in the back yard. See you boys tomorrow. Unfortunately, Claire can't make it. I love you both so much."

Jeremy replies immediately. "See you tomorrow, Nana. Lunch sounds delicious. I love you."

I feel myself break into a silly grin as I read his text.

"Oh, how I love my baby boy."

Gazing in the bathroom mirror as I brush my hair, I see Mattie in the reflection. How great it is to be back.

The renewed Mattie has eyes that shine and twinkle and a mouth that slightly curves upward in an all-knowing gentle smile, a smile that declares, "Life is good."

"I'll see my boys tomorrow," I say out loud to the mirror as I finish my nightly bathroom routine.

I nestle down into my bed, listening to my heartbeat, thinking again about both men: my son and my grandson. Both have always been a part of every beat of my heart from the moment they were born. All my children have. Their existence validated my existence and gave my life purpose. I believe most mothers feel that way.

Remembering that I needed to take my evening pills, I reach for my meds that are in the drawer next to that dusty Ruger, briefly dwelling on the dark times that the vision of that weapon conjured up, and also very thankful that the Lord and all my numerous guardian angels watched over me that night so many, many months ago.

As I grab my water glass and pills, I hear my heart thumping loudly in my ears as it starts to race erratically. I grab the edge of the bed to steady myself as I attempt to inhale a full breath of air. "That's odd," I think. "It has to be because I'm excited about lunch tomorrow." Suddenly a sharp pain stabs into my jaw and radiates down my left arm leaving me completely winded, light headed, and very frightened.

Gasping for a solid breath of air, I think, "Crap, am I having a heart attack? No, that can't be happening. I'm just sore and tired from everything I did today." Then, in utter amazement, I watch in slow motion as my water glass slips from my hand and crashes to the floor, shattering on the beautiful hardwood.

"I have to clean up the glass and water," I think. "The water will stain my floor."

The pulsing and thumping in my ears grows louder, as my heart feels like it's going to explode out of my body. Somehow, I manage to reach down for the glass, and as I do, I feel the jagged edge of a shard of glass cut my palm. Looking down at the gaping wound on my hand that immediately starts to bleed profusely, I instantly remembered Jeremy's vision of the lady in the clouds so many years ago. "She is old, with white curly hair, and has red on her hand."

"I'll be damned. Jeremy saw me like this when he was a child. I wonder if he has always had visions. I'll have to remember to ask him tomorrow."

After a few minutes, the pain in my chest begins to subside somewhat, so I get up and head to the medicine cabinet to doctor my wound. I carefully clean and bandage the cut, and then, to be on the safe side, I grab a couple of baby aspirin and swallow them dry.

Shuffling to the closet where I keep my cleaning supplies, I gather the dustpan and broom to clean up the glass.

"Crap, I'm exhausted."

Somehow, I manage to get everything cleaned up and crawl into bed.

In the morning, I am grateful and a bit surprised that my eyes spring open. My chest, however, is somewhat sore, and I am feeling a bit short of breath. I glance at my bedside clock.

"Wow, it's almost 11:00 a.m. My boys will be here in two hours. I need to get going. But do it slowly, woman," I cautioned myself.

I go to the kitchen to make some coffee and check my phone while waiting for it to brew. Ethan finally replied to my text that I sent last night.

"Mom, are you making your étouffée? I can't wait. See you tomorrow. Love you, Mom."

As I sip on my cup of coffee, I remember that I haven't picked up any good bread for lunch. I'll call Ethan to have him pick some up.

While dialing his number, I start to feel slightly dizzy again. I pour my coffee down the sink, thinking it could be the caffeine, and then Ethan answers.

"Hey, son. I forgot to pick up some good crusty bread. Could you get some?" I say breathlessly.

"Sure, that's not a problem. Are you okay, Mom? You don't sound like yourself."

I reply, "I'm okay, just a bit tired. Don't worry. I'll see you and Jeremy in a few hours." Ethan was quiet for a moment and then said, "Mom, do you realize how you have brought our family back together?"

I answer quickly, "Ethan, I never did that. All I did was write my story about what happened to our family. Doing that helped me reclaim my voice and control over my life after it had been taken away by unfortunate circumstances. Jeremy is the one that reached out to us. He is the one that brought us together again."

Ethan answers, "Yeah, you're right. I'll see you in an hour, and I won't forget the bread."

After our call ends, I still feel a bit dizzy, so I grab some more aspirin and swallow them down with some water.

"Hopefully this will make me feel a bit better," I think as I lift the lid off the étouffée to give it a stir. Wow, does it smell delicious!

After turning the burner down to simmer, I head to the bathroom to shower.

As I finish my shower, I notice that the cut on my palm has opened up again. There is a small trail of blood running down my hand. Grabbing some tissue, I apply pressure to the cut, hoping that it will stem the bleeding. I sure don't want to explain to my guys what happened the night before. Throughout my life, I never really told anyone how I truly was feeling, emotionally, physically or mentally, and I wasn't going to start now. If anyone asked, I would always reply, "I'm fine" or "I'm okay." Today would not be any different.

Now dressed, I head back to the kitchen to check on lunch. As I survey my kitchen, I am pleased with what I have accomplished. Everything is nicely organized. The iced tea is made; the bowls, bread plates, glasses, and napkins are out, as well as the utensils. Everything is ready to take out back to the garden table for lunch.

At that point, I decided I'd let the boys take everything out back.

Glancing at the clock, I see it's 12:50 p.m.

Since I have nothing else to do except wait for Ethan and Jeremy, I leisurely head out to the back yard.

Once out back, I glance at the trees in my yard marveling at the sunlit canopy that they create. David and I planted each and every one of those trees many years ago, hoping to develop the canopy that I now admire. Shuffling through the leaves that had already fallen, I take a seat on the bench that he and I bought in remembrance of Mamaw decades ago. It is the same concrete bench carved with hummingbirds, that once sat in the cemetery down south. I love this bench.

Sniffing the air, I can just begin to smell that fall aroma that everyone knows, that earthy smell of things dying that is somehow soothing. To me, on this day, it is a cleansing scent that reminds us that even though all things die, there is always the promise of rebirth in the future.

A breeze picks up, and I pull my sweater more tightly around me. While doing so, I dislodge the tissue on my cut, which pulls the new scab off.

"Crap, it's bleeding again. Why didn't I put a Band-Aid on that before I left the house? You're really losing it, woman."

I wad the old tissue into a ball and place it back on the cut, closing my fist around it, hoping that it will stop the bleeding. But it continues to bleed through the tissue and begins to drip down my hand.

Leaning back on Mamaw's bench, I close my eyes and savor the dappled fall sun as it hits my face through the filter of the colored leaves overhead. It is a wonderful dance of light and dark on my face.

In the distance I hear Ethan and then Jeremy in the house.

"Mom, lunch smells great. Where are you? I brought the bread," Ethan hollers.

Then I hear Jeremy say, "Nana, I've brought you some more chrysanthemums for your garden. Nana, where are you?"

Silly boys, I told them I'd be out back if I wasn't in the house.

"I'm out back, sitting on Mamaw's bench," I whisper.

Through half-closed eyes, I watch my two beautiful boys open up the back door and race toward me in a panic.

"Why are they looking so frantic? Has my étouffée boiled over? No, I put it on simmer. What is wrong with them?"

Suddenly, it dawns on me.

Before I lose final sight of my boys, I catch one last breath and, looking up at them both, whisper to them.

"Thank you for finding me. I'm not lost anymore."